DEAD RIVER

ALSO BY CYN BALOG

Fairy Tale
Sleepless
Starstruck
Touched

DEAD RIVER

CYN BALOG

DELACORTE
PRESS

Text copyright © 2013 by Cyn Balog
Jacket art copyright © 2013 by Paul Knight (tree) and
Adrian Muttitt (background) for Trevillion Images

All rights reserved. Published in the United States by Delacorte Press,
an imprint of Random House Children's Books,
a division of Random House, Inc., New York.

Delacorte Press is a registered trademark and the colophon is a
trademark of Random House, Inc.

randomhouse.com/teens

Educators and librarians, for a variety of teaching tools,
visit us at RHTeachersLibrarians.com

Library of Congress Cataloging-in-Publication Data
Balog, Cyn.
Dead River / Cyn Balog. — 1st ed.
p. cm.
Summary: "A weekend rafting trip turns deadly when ghosts start
turning up . . . and want something from high school senior Kiandra
that she isn't sure she can give them"—Provided by publisher.
ISBN 978-0-385-74158-3 (hc) — ISBN 978-0-375-99012-0 (lib. bdg.)
ISBN 978-0-375-98578-2 (ebook)
[1. Rafting (Sports)—Fiction. 2. Ghosts—Fiction. 3. Death—Fiction.
4. Horror stories.] I. Title.
PZ7.B2138De 2013
[Fic]—dc23
2012005649

The text of this book is set in 12-point Adobe Caslon Pro.
Book design by Heather Daugherty

Printed in the United States of America

10 9 8 7 6 5 4 3 2 1

First Edition

Random House Children's Books supports the First Amendment
and celebrates the right to read.

For Mandy Hubbard
for taking this wild journey with me

ACKNOWLEDGMENTS

Huge thanks go out to my agent, Jim McCarthy, and the whole crew at Random House Children's Books, including my editor, Wendy Loggia. This story wouldn't have been possible without John Anderson, who lured an unsuspecting and completely gutless author on a rafting trip on the Dead River many years ago. Thank you also to Jennifer Murgia, the best cheerleader there is, and to the Debs, for nearly five years of inspiration. Thanks also to my kids, for always keeping my spirits afloat. And never least, my deepest appreciation goes to my husband, who pulls me back onto the raft, time and time again.

PROLOGUE

"**W**ho are you?" I asked, my voice flat. Seven-year-olds are all about blunt. No "Hi, how do you do, nice weather we're having." After all, he was fishing in my spot.

"No one worth knowin'," he said in a gooey Southern twang, turning back to his fishing pole. "Fish're bitin' like mosquitoes on a hog."

I took a step closer. His fishing pole wasn't a nice one like mine. Just a stick with string tied to it. His jeans were holey and dirty, too. He didn't have a shirt; from the color of his skin he was probably one of those boys who went shirtless from May to September. Freckles like tiny coffee beans mingled with the deep russet hue on his shoulders and nose.

I kicked a stone with my big toe. "You're in my spot," I said as the stone skittered off the bright red paint of my dinghy, nicking it.

My spot was the best on the whole Delaware. It was on an island twenty yards off the bank on the Jersey side. The island was big enough for only a couple of shade trees, my cooler of lemonade, and the spot where I'd plant my backside. A lot of times when it rained, it was underwater. But now it wasn't. It was a perfect time for fishing.

He wiggled his toes in the mud, looked around, patted the ground beside him. "Room enough for two."

Just barely. I eyed the spot suspiciously. That was where I usually put my cooler. His backside was where mine usually went. I couldn't tell how old he was; most everyone on my street was so much older than me, they might as well have been from another planet. He was a younger older, though. Maybe only a decade or so older. That made him the most interesting thing I'd seen all day. So I deigned to sit beside him on my mound in the river. "You talk funny," I said.

He laughed. "Way I see it, you're the one talking funny, kid."

I gave him a big "hmph" and cast my line. He watched my every move, silently, like a cat, until his string began to bob. He pulled a big fat silver beauty out of the water and grabbed it in his hands as its tail swished back and forth, painting dots of midnight blue on his faded denim. Then he smiled and let it go.

"What did you do that for?" I asked.

"Don't eat fish," he answered.

"Then why catch them?"

He shrugged. "Somethin' to pass the time."

I shook my head. "There're a lot funner ways to pass the time, if you don't eat fish."

He chuckled. "Well, kid, if you must know, I'm waitin' on someone."

"Oh yeah? Who?"

"A missus. She'll be along in a shake."

"A what?" When he didn't answer, I asked, "Your girl-friend?"

"Nah." His fishing line bobbed again. He pulled in another one, silver and beautiful. The fish dangled from the fraying, sad excuse for a line as he inspected it closely, smiling with pride. I looked at my own rod, glittering red in the sun, a present from my mother for my birthday. The sinker floated on the water, still.

"Well, she's not taking my spot," I muttered as he tossed the fish back. "You're just catching the same fish over and over again. What bait you using?"

"Just some worms and bugs I dug up." He looked at my pole. "You ain't gonna catch nothin' with that gleamin' piece of horse manure. The fish'll spot that thing a mile away."

"I do just fine," I said, even though I hadn't caught anything with it yet. My fishing spot had always been good to me, but not lately. I'd been thinking that maybe it was a cursed pole, since I'd gotten a paper cut on the wrapping when I opened it. "I may be a girl, but I know plenty about fishing."

He shrugged again. "You underestimate them fish," he said with a snicker. "Fish're suspicious creatures, kid."

Know-it-all. And that was stupid. Fish, suspicious? Fish are dumb. About as dumb as he sounded.

His line bobbed again. I wanted to punch him. Instead, I just wrinkled my nose at him. Then I got my pole, stuffed it in my dinghy, and grabbed my oars. "You could give whatever you catch to my family. We eat fish. Which is what you're supposed to do with them."

"Maybe so, maybe so. You going, girl?"

"Yeah. You're in my spot." I sighed heavily, hoping he wouldn't decide he liked my spot enough to frequent it. Then I pointed at my house on the bank. "I live in that white house over there. Where do you live?"

He didn't seem interested, didn't even bother looking toward where my finger pointed. "Other side of the river."

"In Pennsylvania?"

He nodded at the tree-lined bank as if it had just been introduced to him. "That where that is?" Then he smiled. In all my days on this earth I would never forget that smile. The hot summer sun paled in comparison. "Yeah. Pennsylvania."

"Wait. How'd you get here, without a boat?"

He laughed. "Swam."

"No way. The current?"

"I'm a powerful good swimmer, kid. Current's no match for a powerful good swimmer like me."

I raised my eyebrows. My parents would never let me out in the middle of the river like that. The island was as far as I was allowed to venture, because even when it was rough, the water was barely up to my waist. "Oh. Well. You ever catch any fish you want to give me, I'm right over there," I said slowly, pointing the way to my house again. But he didn't bother to turn. He just stared at the ripples in the water. His line began to bob again. I couldn't stand it.

"Sorry," he said, shaking his head. "Can't."

I fought back the urge to shove him as he pulled another big beauty in. "Why not? Are you some kind of fish-loving wacko or something?"

"'Cause I don't go over there." He looked at me, the corners of his mouth hanging low. That was another thing I'd always remember. That look. Not frightening. Sad. More than sad. Regretful. "Not unless I have to."

Turned out I didn't have to worry about him taking up permanent residence on my fishing spot. I suppose he found who he was waiting for and moved on, just like the river, never settling in one place for too long.

CHAPTER ONE

Row row row your boat
and please please please take me
gently down the stream
to where I can't be hurt. We'll go
merrily merrily merrily merrily
and I won't fight
for life is but a dream
and death I think is the awakening.

Have you ever heard of suicide by river? You just wade out deeper and deeper, and before long the current carries you away. And by then there is nothing you can do about it.

A lot of people wonder what goes through a person's mind during the moments they're pulled away. Do they regret those steps into the churning waves? Do their lungs burn as they gulp for air and get nothing but earthy, thick liquid instead?

I don't wonder, though. Because wondering means I'd have

to start thinking of *her*. And I won't spend a second thinking of someone who didn't think of me.

"You're zoning," a voice calls me back. Justin. One of his arms is draped over the steering wheel, and for the first time I realize his other arm is around me. He drums his thick fingers on my shoulder.

I give him a smile. "No, I'm not."

"Then what was the last thing I said?"

"The river is going to be outrageous," I answer.

That's only a guess, but a safe one, since all winter he's been talking about this trip and how the river is going to be outrageous. He keeps fidgeting the foot that's not on the gas pedal. Justin likes outdoorsy things, like climbing mountains and sleeping under the stars in subzero temperatures. He's been going to dam releases on the Dead since he was eleven. He's wearing a red-and-black-check lumberjack shirt, for God's sake. How did we ever get together? I much prefer sleeping in a warm bed. Hot cocoa. Icy water *not* dripping off the end of my nose. I'm, like Jack says in *Titanic,* more of an "indoor girl." Nothing wrong with that.

Though I should probably *not* be thinking about freezing waves and peril in the water right now.

"You write a good poem?" he asks me as I close the cover of the little leather-bound book I carry everywhere.

I wrinkle my nose. I'm never sure anything I write is good. I'm the editor of the yearbook and literary magazine only because nobody else wanted those jobs. Wayview High is big into hockey, and that's about it. My school puts out only one issue of its literary magazine, *The Comet,* a year, mostly because we get no submissions, and so half of the poems in this year's issue were from me. I'd even written a few haiku *about* hockey, hoping it would get someone's, anyone's, interest. Little good it did. I'm not sure anyone read them, other than my English teacher. Oh, and Justin. At least he said he did. But looking down at my most recent effort, I'm not sure if I want anyone to see it. "Please take me gently down the stream to where I can't be hurt"? Somehow I can't escape the thought of icy cold water and death, even in my writing.

"Are you scared?" Justin asks me.

"No," I say quickly, resolute. "Of course not." At least, I try to sound resolute, but it's hard, especially since the thought that's now center stage in my brain is that of a thousand human icicles bobbing in a black, endless sea.

"Of course you are, Ki. This is the Dead River we're talking about," Hugo Holbrook says from the back of the truck. I dig my fingers into the vinyl armrest. Of all the people my cousin Angela could have invited on this trip, I can't believe it's Hugo I'll be sleeping in a cramped cabin with for four nights. It's bad enough that I have to spend hours after school in the closet-sized yearbook office with him when we're on deadline. How does she find him even remotely attractive? He has nostrils like black holes and eyes so close together that the space between them is a rickety footbridge.

And I'm convinced that his laugh is why earplugs were invented. *Wahah wahah wahah.* "Look at her. She's shaking."

"It's freaking cold," I mutter, grimacing at Angela, Miss He's-Kind-of-Cute-and-Really-Likes-Me, in the rearview mirror. She's the same cousin who nursed a frighteningly ugly and smelly three-legged lizard back to health in her bedroom when we were eight, after my aunt and uncle ran it over with their Cadillac SUV. Most people wouldn't have touched it with the back of a shovel, but Angela let it sleep on her pillow.

But Angela doesn't notice my scowl. Her eyes are focused on the river. It's black and churning because they released the dam yesterday, something they do about ten times a year so that the rapids will be intense for rafting. Not exactly as inviting as, say, a dance floor. And lucky me, I'll be in the middle of it tomorrow.

We pass a wooden sign in a stark field: WHAT A MAN SOWS THAT SHALL HE ALSO REAP—GALATIANS 6:7. I shudder and avert my eyes. I'd actually convinced myself that I wanted this. That this would be fun. The sparkling white frost in the bottom of a roadside ditch makes me think about the ice-blue satin gown I saw in Macy's. Then Angela says, "Turn here."

She points down a narrow dirt road descending into the thick forest.

"You're not going down there," I say, incredulous, as Justin barrels in. It's clear, of course, that he is, that we all are, but

I think the visions of white water are dancing through his head, crowding out all the sane thoughts.

"Why not?"

"Hello? Mud season?" Among other things. It looks so dark and final down that road. As in *People have gone in, but they've never come out.*

"That's what four-wheel drive is for," he says, shifting into gear. The engine revs and we push forward. He pats the dashboard. "That a boy, Monster." Justin always wanted a dog, so since his parents forbade it, he named his truck Monster.

"It's cool, Ki." Angela smiles and pounds her fists on her thighs. "Come on, Monster. You can do it!"

I shiver again, thinking that if my aunt and uncle, Angela's parents, didn't own a cabin in Caratunk, we never would have considered coming here. But Justin, Angela, and I have been planning this forever. Well, mostly Justin and Angela. They've talked about it constantly. It was Justin's idea. Instead of going to the prom, we would skip school and drive up to the cabin for a long weekend during the release. The two of them were so into it, and so anti-prom, that I didn't want to be the brat to tell them I thought dressing up for one evening might be fun. Of course, since I thought my dad would freak out if I even mentioned the word "river" to him, I told Justin we'd have to lie. I didn't explain the details to Justin, just that my father thought rafting was dangerous. So we decided to tell my dad that we were going camping at Baxter State Park. Justin hates deceiving anyone, so for him to lie to my father so convincingly, I knew this was where his heart was.

Back when the idea was hatched, I'd convinced myself I didn't care about the prom. My friends had a way of rolling their eyes and making snide jokes about the event every time it was mentioned, so I went along with it. Angela is a flip-flops and T-shirt girl, so she was dying for an excuse to dodge tripping in three-inch heels. Plus, she's been on the Dead a hundred times. I'd always seen myself in ice-blue satin, descending a long, winding staircase with a tuxedoed prince, but I couldn't tell them that. They would have laughed their heads off at me.

You reap what you sow, I think, leaning my forehead against the cool window, letting my breath condense on it in a circle so I can draw a smiley face. Then I wipe it out as Monster sticks again and Angela shrieks, "Just gun it! Gun it, boy!" like a total hick.

I *so* sowed this.

It's too late now. I should have said something to Justin. Something like "I'll go rafting with you if you go to the prom with me." After all, the heart of com*prom*ise is *prom.* But this weekend is all him. And it's too late to change that. I'll just need to suck it up, pretend I'm enjoying myself, and make him take me shopping next weekend. This weekend can be his, as long as the next one is mine.

Justin grins, digs his foot into the accelerator, and we lurch forward. More shrieking. Laughter. This morning's cinnamon raisin bagel gurgles in the back of my throat. I'm not even in the water yet and I can already feel the current carrying me away.

A minute later the cabin comes into view, and my spirits brighten considerably.

"Whoa, Angela. You said 'cabin'?" Justin asks, staring up at it.

"Yeah. Cozy, huh?"

My mouth drops open. Justin, Hugo, and I live in trailers on the west end of Wayview, Maine. It should be called Noview, though, because everywhere you look, there's nothing but tall pines. It was Dad's way of insulating me from anything that could possibly remind me of the river where my mother died. There's not a brook, a pond, or even a puddle anywhere in sight. Angela's house, or *mansion,* as most would say, is on the east end of the forest. Angela's dad, my uncle, is a retired CEO and owns a lot of real estate. This vacation "cabin," which they bought last year but have maybe used a total of twice, is probably bigger than all three of our trailers put together. I look over at Justin, and for once, his expression matches mine.

Then he sighs. I am sure he was looking forward to "roughing it." I'm feeling better already. I can keep my distance from Hugo. Maybe we'll even have running water. A steamy shower would be so . . .

She catches me smiling. "It's nice, huh? But my parents turned off the water for the winter, so . . ."

Of course. They only use the cabin in the warmer months. The pipes would have frozen and burst during the long

Maine winter if they hadn't turned off the water. I swallow the bad taste in my throat. "It's cool."

We pile out and Justin begins pulling things from the bed of his truck. Groceries, a backpack of my clothes, my travel chess set, the liter of Absolut Justin took from his dad's overstocked and underused liquor cabinet to celebrate our conquering of the Dead. Hugo starts snapping pictures of all the trees, as if we don't have enough of them back home. From here, the river sounds like the gentle hum of an electric toothbrush. The sky is the somber color of castle walls, and the leaves turn out, welcoming rain. Shapeless heaps of dingy snow fight for survival in the new spring grass. Angela grabs a handful of snow and molds it into a ball.

"Don't you dare," I whisper, shivering as I back away.

But it's obvious she has other plans. She launches it over to Justin. It breaks into pieces squarely at the back of his neck, making him jump. He turns to us, amused, but before I can point her out, I realize Angela is already pointing at me, an innocent expression on her face. "Dude, I know it's you," he says to Angela.

He throws my pillow at her. It lands in the mud. "Justin!" I shout, annoyed, but I stop when I realize everyone else is laughing. Sometimes it bothers me how well the two of them get along. After all, they are best friends, and have known each other since way before I came into the picture. Justin once told me that Angela is like the sister he never had, and physically she's not at all like the long line of fair, willowy blondes he's been associated with, of which I'm the latest. She's not fat, but she's solid, with wild, curly black hair and dark skin that turns almost chocolate in the sun. Angela was afraid that she would feel like a third wheel on this trip, which is why she invited Hugo, but she and Justin have so much in common, sometimes *I* feel like the odd person out.

I've heard the story a thousand times. They met on a skiing trip at Sugarloaf when they were both trying to learn the bunny slope. Their parents became friends and then they found out that they both lived in Wayview, so they kept in touch, going on vacations together sometimes in the winter and summer. Angela went to a private school in Massachusetts, but when I came up, my father insisted I go to the public school, mostly because we didn't have the money. Justin was in my class, but I didn't know him well. When we reached high school, Angela successfully convinced her parents to transfer her to public school by failing out of every class she took. Her parents thought that with my father teaching at Wayview High, maybe she'd be inclined to goof off less. Freshman year, she introduced me to Justin, but I didn't think anything of it other than that he was really cute. He was dating some other blonde in our class, but we always seemed to get thrown together when Angela had parties. It wasn't until junior year, when I had to do an article on the swim team for yearbook, that we fell for each other. He was the captain, and he came by the yearbook office one day after school to identify all the people in the group photo. He was leaning over me, really close, and then he just moved in and kissed me. We made out for an hour, right in the yearbook office. I remember constantly saying, "But Angela . . . ," and him whispering, "Angela has nothing to do with this."

I snatch the pillow up and dust it off. It's not that bad. I feel stupid for overreacting. Hugo confirms the fact by snapping a picture of me and captioning it "Girl About to Explode." He grins. "Not like there probably aren't four thousand pillows in this place."

I push the camera out of my face. I'm about to explain that my pillow is hypoallergenic and my allergies are always worst in the spring and it's the only pillow I've found that's comfortable enough, but he's right. I do need to loosen up. Funny, I've spent so much energy trying to convince my dad that he'd be okay if he took the shackles off my wrists that I never even thought about whether *I* would be okay once I finally got loose. This is my first trip away from my dad, away from home. And that is thrilling . . . but terrifying.

I stifle a sneeze, then cross my arms over my chest, pinching my skin and mentally reciting my motto: *You will be chill. Ice cubes will be jealous of you.*

I'm about to pick up my backpack from Justin's feet but stop when I see something in the woods. The curve of an elbow, pale white against the lush green, still and stark among the new leaves as they sway in the wind. But the next second, it's gone. I suck in a breath, exhale slowly. The last thing I need to be doing is seeing things. Again.

The thing is, nobody here knows about my mother. Not even Angela. Hell, *I* don't really even know. The mystery Nia Levesque became a part of is five hundred miles away, and I'd like it to stay there. Nobody here knows my history. And I'm going to keep it that way.

CHAPTER TWO

It's been almost ten years since I moved into the tall pines of Wayview, Maine, the last place on earth I'd have picked to live, if it was up to me.

Unfortunately, it wasn't.

So I guess that means it will be the tenth anniversary of my mom's death. Not that I'm keeping track. We left New Jersey only a couple weeks afterward, and we've never been back.

These are the facts I have: Nia Levesque waded into the Delaware River one fair summer's night shortly after my seventh birthday. I know little else because how much a person's mother hated life is not something people like to discuss with a seven-year-old. I remember things, though, like that her skin was always damp and clammy and that her hair always looked like it needed a comb run through it. Despite those things, she was my sun. When she was gone, it was like my whole universe went out of orbit, because I'd been so used to following three steps behind her.

I've heard that after a suicide, the people left behind always look back and see signs in the victim, signs of pain or trauma they somehow ignored. I know I was only seven, but with my mom, there were no indications. Nothing. She was never distant; she smiled and hugged and kissed me all the time. When I look back at my mom, I can't help but think there was so much about her I didn't know, so much she must have kept hidden from me.

I know that I have forgotten things: the slope of her nose, the color of her skin, the exact blue shade of her eyes, the little mannerisms she had. Pictures don't convey a whole person, and I only have one of those. It wasn't the one I would have chosen, but I didn't know that my father and I would never return home. I would have taken my whole photo book, which had countless beautiful pictures of my mother, but he chose one picture, from my sixth birthday. In it, she's not even smiling. She's leaning over me as I blow out the candles on my birthday cake and she looks worried, probably that a lock of my hair might get caught in the flame. I don't know what her smile looks like anymore. Every memory I have is just a poor reproduction, merely a shade of her. I worry that as days go by I will forget more and more, and the only thing left will be this overwhelming feeling of abandonment. That and the worried, uneasy woman she was in that picture.

When we lived in New Jersey, we had a house right on the river. I had the best room, all pink, and the sunrise would bounce off the waves and create magical iridescent ripples on my walls. My father put glow-in-the-dark stars on the ceiling, but when the moon shone, it would splash the brightest white ripples right onto them. More often than not, I felt like I was sleeping underwater rather than under a night sky.

Strange things happened around the time of her death. I can't really explain it. I would lie in my bed, listening to the rush of the river against the rocks, and in time it would sound like voices. Whispering to me. Then the visions came. They didn't start off frightening. I'd lie in the dark with my eyes open, watching them parade through my room, oblivious to me, a series of who-knows-what—ideas or dreams or ghosts, playing on a movie reel. Redheaded boys in overalls, fishing. Girls in old-fashioned swim trunks, holding their noses as they plunged into the blackness. Men in waders, sleeves rolled up. Sometimes I'd have conversations with them, play games with them, but usually I'd just watch them quietly, all night long, wishing I could be part of their care-free, happy lives.

Until the images . . . changed.

I fight back the picture of the girl in the pink party dress and tight, stringy braids. I didn't know her name, didn't know anything about her except that her expression was hopeless and sad, she was covered in dirt, one of her knee-high socks was pooled around her ankle, and her knees were bloody. I think she wanted to tell me something, but whenever she opened her mouth to speak to me, mud poured from it. Mud trickled from her nose, covering the lower part of her face like a beard. Her cheeks were muddy and lined with tears.

I stopped sleeping. My dad was stressed out enough teaching history to inner-city kids in Paterson, in a district two hours from our house, so he didn't need me screaming bloody murder in the middle of the night, like I so often did. He thought I missed my mom. And yeah, I did, but there was more. And I was afraid to tell him. Turned out I was as good at keeping secrets as my mom was.

I lost so many things from that room. My fairy brush, my favorite blue hair ties, my stuffed zebra. And every picture of my mother, except for one. One day, my dad took me out for what I thought was ice cream but turned out to be forever. He'd hastily packed a bag with only a few of my clothes, and so I lost my brand-new Cinderella T-shirt and my comfortable jeans. I don't know why we left so quickly. Luckily, he'd said, he had family up in Wayview, with a kid just my age, and he couldn't wait for me to meet them. I knew my father was anxious, because when he is, he repeats himself. As we drove, he kept telling me, over and over again, how much I'd like Maine. How Aunt Missy and Uncle Jim and Angela couldn't wait to see me. How I was his "everything." That's the thing I remember the most, "You're my everything," spouted out again and again until it didn't mean anything. I didn't care. I had to pee so bad but kept thinking we were almost there. With every passing mile, I became more and more certain I'd never see my things, my old house, again. And I couldn't stop thinking that if Mom were here, she wouldn't have agreed to this. She hated the cold. I realized then that this was the first of many things she wouldn't be around to protect me from.

That was when I started to hate her. Not long after, I stopped asking questions about why she did what she did. My father always changed the subject anyway.

Last year Angela hooked up with this guy named Spee. Ken Specian, really, but everyone called him Spee. He was a big jock, totally full of himself, which tells you how much I liked him. Angela has the worst luck with guys; watching her trying to get on with a guy she's really into is like watching a plane attempting to touch down without landing gear. Anyway, she was so into Spee, but it was obvious that he didn't give a rat's you-know-what about her, because, well, he never took her out in public. He never took her anywhere they might see other people from school. All they ever did was go to Frank's Diner, ten miles out of town on this deserted mountain road. Angela would just mention Frank's and I would know what she was up to. It was a place the toothless crowd frequented, so she and Spee brought the average age of the customers down to ninety.

But then, after three months of meeting her there every week, he just stopped calling her. Angela never said as much, but I know she was devastated, because two months later she finally convinced me to go with her to Frank's. "I need to see our place one last time. To prove he has no hold over me," she told me. So we went. It was completely uncomfortable, sitting among dozens of people who had to put their dentures on the paper advertisement place mats to keep them clean while they nursed their free senior citizen coffees. But we did it, and there was no mistaking the look of triumph on Angela's face when we paid our bill and stepped outside.

That's kind of what this trip is like to me. I think my dad thinks I'll have a mental breakdown if I see another river. Maybe because that's what he would do. But not me. This weekend, I'm proving that the river, that my mother, has no hold over me. She hasn't been here when I needed her, so there's no way I'll let her dictate where I can and can't go. She lost that privilege ten years ago.

And seriously, I'm fine. More than fine, now that I'm out of the Monster. I inhale the crisp, clean scent of pine and feel just perfect.

Angela bounds over to the front porch and pokes around in a snow-covered planter for the key. She and I never talk about my mom. I know Angela never met her, and I don't think my aunt or uncle did, either, so there really isn't anything they could say. I think someone told Angela my mom was sick. My mom sometimes complained of not feeling well. Headaches, usually. She tried to hide that from me, too, but I was lost without her, so I'd often sit outside her bedroom, waiting for the Excedrin to kick in. She had a giant green vat of headache pills in the medicine cabinet and a little matching one in her purse. I guess the whole illness thing was the way to go if you wanted to avoid the "uncomfortable truth." Which, really, everyone did.

Inside the "cabin," there's a three-story-high stone fireplace decorated with giant moose antlers. Uncle Jim loves the outdoors, too, but he's no Davy Crockett. He is all about modern conveniences. Their place in Wayview, while full of big windows that bring the outdoors in, is crammed with all the latest gadgets: space-age coffeemakers that do everything but pour the stuff down your throat, wall-sized televisions, things like that. I should have known this place would be no different. Angela catches me looking and says, "The antlers are fake."

"Oh," I say, wondering where people buy fake moose antlers. There are paintings of mountain and forest scenes everywhere and it smells like pine, not real pine like outside, but pine air freshener. Something about it inspires me. There's a poem in here somewhere. I pull out my trusty notebook and scribble some notes: *What is real? What is good about nature anyway?*

Justin looks around, his upper lip curled in disdain. It's not exactly the great outdoors. He turns to me and laughs. "Well, aren't we just glowing?"

I smile. "Oh yes. I'm going to go pick out my bedroom. Do you think it has a fireplace? Maybe a robe and fuzzy slippers?"

"What are you writing?" he asks.

"Notes. Observations. 'My boyfriend's upper lip disappears completely when he is disappointed.'"

He realizes what he's doing and sticks out his lips, moving them up and down like a fish gulping for air. "This better? Ah, well. And here I thought we would get the chance to snuggle."

He's mocking me. I'm always cold, so *I'm* the one usually

trying to snuggle against *him*. I punch his shoulder as we climb the open staircase to the loft.

Angela follows us upstairs and leads us to a giant room with another fireplace and a huge brass king bed. "You can have the master suite, if you want," she says, giving me a wink.

We throw our stuff onto the bed. It's not really a big deal, having the master suite to ourselves for a weekend. Teaching AP history and supervising three extracurriculars, Dad can't always be around to watch us. At my house, we could have wild monkey sex every afternoon on the kitchen table if we so chose. As it happens, we don't choose that, ever. I know of people in my class who live under their parents' thumbs, so the second they're free, they're going at it, in public restrooms, parks, wherever. Justin and I aren't like that. We never were.

Not that I have much to compare him to. Justin dated a bunch of other girls before me. I don't think I ever saw him single. But Justin is my first boyfriend. So when we started dating, there were a lot of things I didn't know. But we've been together since freshman year. Now being with him is like sliding into a favorite T-shirt.

And yet somehow, I think as I pull my long underwear out of my bag, *I still couldn't tell him I wanted to go to the prom.*

Maybe because, after three years, he should have just known.

Angela walks back down the hallway, whistling something that sounds like a cross between "Let's Get It On" and

"Zip-a-Dee-Doo-Dah." Justin puts his arms around me. He looks around and sighs.

"I know, you wanted to toast marshmallows over an open fire," I say.

He nods. "Yeah."

"Fine," I say, thinking, *Next weekend. Next weekend we're going shopping, come hell or high water.* And high water is definitely coming, whether I like it or not. He can handle a couple of hours holding my bag as I try on new clothes. "It's pretty warm tonight. You and I can go out in our sleeping bags and light a fire and sleep under the stars. Okay?"

He raises his eyebrows. "You'd hate that."

"No, it'll be . . . fun."

He laughs, because I'm sure my face must be twisted in disgust. "I knew I loved you for a reason."

"Besides, Hugo's really getting on my nerves. It will be nice to get away from him."

"He just makes fun of you all the time because he wants you," he says matter-of-factly.

I try to swat him away. Justin is always under the impression that anything with a Y chromosome is after me. This includes priests, dogs, and old men with walkers. "What? Oh please."

"What can I say? You're hot. Especially in that getup." I start to look down at my boring North Face jacket, which is the exact opposite of hot, but he pulls me back and hugs me tighter. Hugging him feels right, comfortable, like my pillow. "Besides, he's a guy. And I know what guys are thinking."

"Oh, right." I've heard this one before. "Sex, twenty-five hours a day."

"Yep. We basically want to nail anything female. Especially when she's hot."

"This is very comforting news, coming from my boyfriend," I mutter. I might be alarmed if he didn't tell me this anytime I get any attention whatsoever from a member of the opposite sex. Usually with a nudge-nudge and a *See-I-told-you-so* smirk of satisfaction. "So why aren't you trying to get some right now?"

"Because duh. I am a *gentleman.* Obviously." He pats my butt to show me just how chivalrous he is.

"Oh. *Obviously.*"

"Well, the important thing is not that we're thinking of sex with every girl in the world. Because, trust me, we are. The important thing is that we don't act on it."

"Ah, I see," I say, as if we're discussing the theory of relativity. "So this is proven? All guys? Sex all the time?"

"Ask any guy. Go ahead. Ask Hugo."

I cringe. If Hugo is thinking about sex with me, I really would rather not know. "I'll just take your word for it."

We both turn toward the large picture window. I can make out the black water through the trees. It's not far away. For a moment I'm in my old pink bedroom, watching the ripples dance on the walls. Then I think of that little girl, the one dressed in pink. She opens her mouth and the filth begins to ooze over her bottom lip just as I'm jolted back to reality.

"You okay?" Justin asks. When I look at him, confused, he says, "You're shivering. Come on, Hugo's not that bad."

"No, it's not that."

"What, then? Look, you don't have to spend the night outside with me," he says, stroking my cheek softly with the calloused pad of his thumb.

"No, I wasn't—" I begin, but it's better he doesn't know what I was really thinking. About that life that he knows nothing about. It's not worth explaining anyway. The past belongs in the past. This trip is all about moving on, and that's exactly what I plan to do.

CHAPTER THREE

My cell rings while I'm pulling on my long underwear. I check the display and see a familiar number. "Hey, Dad," I say, watching Justin do a little jig by the window. He's so excited by the river, he's gotten dance fever.

"Hey," my dad says. "Where are you?"

"Just got to Baxter," I lie as Justin turns to watch me. I plant my butt on the edge of the bed. "We're setting up our tents now."

"Cool," my dad says. "How's the charge on your phone?"

"It's fine," I say as Justin twirls around the room like he's Julie Andrews in *The Sound of Music*. Totally sexy.

"Mount Katahdin is *breathtaking*! The hills really are alive up here!" Justin shouts. Then he falls down on the ground. Then he pretends that something is attacking him. He gets up, runs, and falls, and by then I guess the imaginary thing is on top of him because he collapses onto his stomach and screams. "And they're . . . going . . . to eat me!"

Shut up, I mouth, but my dad must have heard. "How is Justin?"

"Um, he's . . . ," I begin, watching him miraculously revive.

Justin calls out, "Going to wait until *after* dinner to murder your daughter."

I reach over and smack him. ". . . good."

"Are you okay? Do you need anything? If you do, just call. Just call me anytime. Let your old man know how things are going."

I sigh. That's my dad. By now Justin is making funny faces at me, trying to get me to laugh. He almost succeeds when he rolls his eyes back in his head and pushes up his nose to look like a pig. "Everything's fine. And I've got to go. We're going to the store. We forgot . . ." I look around but can't come up with anything. I'm terrible at thinking on my feet like this.

Justin offers, "Beef jerky?"

I'm about to say it, but I catch myself in time and smack him on the shoulder again. "I mean, we're going on a hike. And we want to get up there before it gets dark."

"*You're* a beef jerky," I whisper at Justin.

"Now?" my dad says. I can just picture him in the living room, looking at the kitchen clock through his bifocals and shaking his head. "It's awful late for that. Bring flashlights in case you're not back by nightfall."

"Don't worry, Mr. Levesque. Everything's fine," Justin calls, starting to make faces again.

I smack him again as I disconnect from my father and sigh. "I hate having to lie to him."

"He's being irrational. People who don't know the facts are quick to condemn it, but white-water rafting is completely safe," Justin says, sounding like a public service announcement. Then he grins. "Now let's go outside!"

We don't get to ditch Hugo after all. While we're gathering our bags and trying to sneak down the stairs, Angela comes out of her room, her eyes big and round. She has eyes that would make the most hardened criminal confess and beg for mercy. They should be surrounded by a nun's wimple. "Where are you off to?"

"We were just, um . . ." Justin looks at me. He's terrible at confrontations.

"We thought we would camp outside. Just for tonight," I explain.

"*You?*" she says to me, incredulous. When I nod, her eyes get wider yet. "But you can't leave me alone with Hugo!" she whispers. "That would be so . . . awkward."

"You invited him," I point out. "What happened to 'He's kind of cute'?"

"Yeah, well, he is, but . . ." Pleading, she looks at Justin. "I don't even really know him that well. Being alone with him *all night,* would be totally *awkward,* with a capital *A.*"

"This is a little plusher than I thought, Angela," Justin says. "Don't get me wrong. It's nice. I just thought that . . ."

She clamps her hand around mine. "We were going to

make popcorn and s'mores and tell scary stories and stuff. *Please*."

Right. Angela was a Girl Scout. She lives for s'mores and scary stories by firelight. I look back at Justin. He clears his throat. "Well, why don't you guys come with us?" he asks.

"Really?" she asks. "Okay! That would be cool!"

She scampers off to gather her things as I glare at Justin. He has this way of caving under the slightest amount of pressure. He squeezes my hand. "It'll be fun," he whispers.

"But . . . Hugo," I say, since that name alone is an explanation as to why it won't be.

He doesn't answer, just takes my sleeping bag from me, as if carrying it is his way of apologizing. Then he leads us out to the backyard. Angela points the way to an old campsite and we set up there. There's a fire pit, and Justin, the master woodsman, finds a way to get a fire burning within a few minutes. When we lay out our sleeping bags, Angela begins to divvy up the marshmallows, graham crackers, and chocolate bars.

When I sit down on my bag, my butt thuds painfully against the hard ground and some insect skitters across my nose. Even with the fire burning and my hands in the pockets of my jacket, my fingertips feel numb. I immediately regret being so sweet to Justin. Not only that, but tomorrow we'll be on the river, instead of getting ready for prom. I was already being nice to him by agreeing to come on this trip. What made me agree to sleep outdoors?

"Scary story time," Angela says. "I am so going first. I've been practicing this one ever since we started planning the trip. It'll totally freak you out, Ki."

I stare at her. "Thanks?"

"No, you'll appreciate this one."

I think she's saying this because I'm a horror movie junkie. But that's indoors, in a well-lit room. Even with Justin to protect me, it's spooky, and we'll be sleeping here all night. Outside the circle, the forest is black. The rushing river sounds like eerie whispers. No, no. The river is fine. The sound is relaxing. *The river has no hold over me.*

"Once upon a time," she begins as I nibble on a marshmallow. She leans forward so that the fire casts strange shadows on her face. "There was this boy."

"Ooooh. Scary," Hugo says.

Nobody bothers to laugh or even to look at him, not even Angela, who is too absorbed in her story to notice him. "His name was Jack McCabe. He grew up in a home with his father, who was a lumberjack. His father was also a very evil man who blamed Jack for the death of his wife in childbirth. So he would beat Jack every night if he didn't do everything he was told. He made Jack clean the house, make him meals, tend to the animals, everything. The father would sit there at night, sharpening the blade of his ax on a stone, watching his son. That was all he ever did. *Sleesh . . . sleesh . . . sleesh.*"

Angela makes a high screeching noise, like nails on a chalkboard. I start to roll my eyes but stop when a shiver touches my shoulders.

An owl hoots. There's a chill in the air, a breeze blowing off the river. I hug myself tighter. It certainly isn't Angela's attempt at scaring me that's making me quiver. It's just numbingly cold. But I can't stop. I move closer to Justin and pull his arm around me.

"So as he was growing up, Jack did whatever his father told him to do, or else he knew he'd be beaten or even killed. One of the things he had to do every night was go down to the river and fetch water. This river." She points in the general direction of the Dead. "He had to go every night, several times, to fill his bucket with water. It was a worn path, lit only by the moon."

"So . . . where was Jill during all this?" Hugo asks.

"I'm trying to tell a story!" Angela says, pouting.

I look up at the moon, the pine needles crisscrossing over it like cat scratches. And then something catches in me. Something familiar. The moon isn't full now, but *then* it was.

Something happened by the light of the full moon.

I swallow, but my throat is dry. The sense of déjà vu creeps over me entirely and for a moment I feel like I'm falling. *Get ahold of yourself, Ki!* I shake it away, steady myself against Justin's broad frame, and try to concentrate on the flames licking at a charred log in the fire pit.

Hugo smiles smugly and pretends to zip his lip as Angela continues. "Anyway, one night as he's walking to fetch water, he sees a girl on the other side of the river. She's crying. He thinks it must be a ghost, as it disappears right away. But then he sees her again, calling to him, always crying and calling to him from the other side of the river. So he follows her. And then he loses sight of her, fetches the water, and goes back home. Every night, he sees the crying girl and follows her, trying to find out what she is, why she is so sad, but every night she disappears, and every night he ends up spending more time outside. His father decides something is going on and so he follows him one night. And as Jack is walking down the path after the girl he hears it. *Sleesh . . . sleesh . . . sleesh.* His father sharpening his ax."

The shivers again. But why? It's a stupid story. And Angela's voice is way too perky and cute to pull it off.

But the moon. That full moon. I can see it now.

And now I can hear the sound of the bucket swinging in Jack's hand. I hear a body moving through the brush, and the footsteps trudging down that worn path to the river. To the Dead.

Sleesh . . . sleesh . . . sleesh.

Now my entire body is alive with tingles. That sound. That slicing sound. I've heard it before. Somewhere.

It's not just coming from Angela. It's everywhere, all around the woods, *echoing in my head.*

He looks up. The blade is silver, glistening in the moonlight slashing down through the leaves. . . .

"He looks around but doesn't see anyone, so he runs to get the water."

Why? Why did you . . . I did everything you asked of me.

Angela pauses for dramatic effect and then whispers, "The last thing he saw was the blade of the ax—"

"Stop!" I say, jumping to my feet. The three of them stare up at me. Hugo has a satisfied expression on his face, like a wuss. I point to a crumpled plastic bag by Angela's feet. "Um. I mean, are there any more marshmallows?"

Amused, she kicks the bag over to me. Like she knows she scared the crap out of me. But she didn't. She wouldn't have, except . . . "Sure," she says. "Knock yourself out."

I grab a handful and snuggle closer to Justin. "That was a lame story," Hugo says. "I give it a C for creativity."

Angela says, "What? It's not creative. It really happened! I read about it in an old book. *Ghost Stories of the Rivers* or something. Jack McCabe supposedly still haunts the river where he died, with the crying girl he was following that night."

Their laughs, dulled by the sound of an ax being sharpened, echo in my head. I try to clamp my hands over my ears but it doesn't help. Justin says something that I can't hear and Angela nods. "It's an old legend from around these parts. They say that when you're about to die, the dead will call to you from the other side of the river. And then when your time is up . . . they come to take you away."

Hugo says, "I've heard that. Kind of like Charon and the river Styx."

"Exactly," Angela answers.

I try to find some moisture in my mouth but it feels like sandpaper. "Um. Can we do something more fun? Maybe sing songs? Fall face-first into the fire?"

"No, wait," Justin says, oblivious to me. Maybe it's a good

thing that he doesn't notice what a scaredy-cat I am, because it means I'm playing it off well. But then he says, "I have a good story. One that we told in fifth-grade camp."

"Fifth-grade camp stories are never good," Hugo says with his annoying laugh, only this time it doesn't sound so annoying. In fact, I think I want to kiss him.

"True," I agree, maybe a little too readily.

"This one is classic," Justin says. "Trust me."

"But I thought we could talk a little about the rafting trip tomorrow. You know, so I'm prepared," I say.

Justin squints at me. I know what he's thinking. I haven't wanted to talk about rafting at all, when it's been his favorite topic of conversation for the past three months. So why this sudden intense interest?

"I *am* a little nervous," I tell him. Which is the truth. Plus, it hides the bigger truth: that something really weird just happened. When Angela was telling her story, I could hear all the sounds in my head: the blade being sharpened, the rusty pail swinging as the boy walked. I could see the ax. Well, maybe not *the* ax, but an ax. But worse than that, I could see the boy lying on the ground, gasping for breath as the blood coursed over his lips, asking, "Why?" *I did everything you asked of me,* he'd choked out before his chest went still. Angela hadn't said anything like that in telling her story. She didn't have to. And yet I knew. It was like I'd been there.

"All right," Justin says. "It's Class Four and Five rapids, meaning it's pretty fierce. But you'll have a blast. Believe me."

I suck in a shot of cold air. I'm not really in the mood for anything *fierce* right now. I want a teddy bear.

He massages my knee. "It's nothing to be nervous about. Like I said, more people—"

"I know, I know. More people get injured going bowling than they do on white-water rafting trips," I say.

"Right. And Ange and I have been on this river a hundred times. We know what to expect."

"Smooth sailing," Ange says. "Totally."

It's true, Angela's and Justin's parents have brought them up here, together, at least once a year since they were in preschool. If any two people know the river inside and out, it's them. Of course, them knowing the river isn't going to save me if I do something stupid, like lose my balance, which is a pretty frequent occurrence. "But what if I fall out of the raft or something?" I ask. "Does that happen?"

He nods. "Sure it does. Sometimes. Rarely. I've been on the river a thousand times and I can count on one hand the number of times I've fallen out. It won't happen to you."

"But if it does?"

"You'll have on your life jacket. And I'll keep you safe," he says, voice firm. "Don't worry."

I nod, because I believe him. Justin doesn't say anything he doesn't mean. He's a simple guy, which is probably the reason I like him so much. Too many of my friends are in relationships with guys who say one thing and do another. And he's completely protective of me, always. One day he'll be a Maine State Police officer, I know. Most people stiffen when they pass a police vehicle because they're afraid of getting a ticket, but he stiffens because he wants to look responsible in case the future officer in charge of hiring is in that police car and might remember Justin five years from now when he interviews for the job.

Just when I think that my efforts to change the subject have worked, Angela pipes up.

"So, Justin. About that story from fifth-grade camp. I want to hear it," she says. I no longer love her. She leans forward. "Go ahead."

I pull my blanket around my body as he begins. I'm hoping I can tune him out. Hoping that he won't choose now to prove that he has the creativity to be a good storyteller. But it's almost as if I'm wearing headphones and his voice is being piped right into my ear. And his voice, which is always kind of soothing, drops to this low, breathy whisper that I've never known him to possess. "Once there was this kid named Trey Vance. He was walking home from school. He wasn't a very big kid, smaller than me . . . maybe Hugo's size, just average. He was taking the shortcut through the woods and there he saw two boys with their backs turned to him. He knew they were older kids from his school who had given him trouble before, so he meant to walk past them quietly. But they turned and saw him, and they suddenly looked all nervous. A few days later the body of a young girl was found at the same location he'd seen the boys, and Trey realized that the older kids must have killed her."

The wind picks up, finding its way to my neckline. I pull

the blanket around me and suddenly it's clear to me. *They'll get him when he goes fishing.*

I don't know how, but suddenly the thought is so clear to me. So obvious, like it's happening right in front of me, right now. I see him tying string to a pole, and beyond him, in a lush forest, a tree branch bends. Someone is watching him. But he is turned away. A lock of dirty-blond hair falls in his eyes and he sweeps it behind his ear, unaware.

Somehow, for some reason, I know more than even *he* does.

"For a few days," Justin goes on, "Trey wrestled with what he'd seen, wondering if he should go to the police. But one of the boys, it turns out, saw Trey as he was running away. So one day Trey was walking to the river, completely unsuspecting."

When Justin mentions the river, suddenly I see the kid at the edge of the pier, in his dirty jeans, with his stick fishing pole. *That's the one. Get him.* I open my mouth, wanting to scream to him, to tell him to watch out. He doesn't know they're behind him. He won't know until it's too late. But I can't find my voice.

Suddenly I can't breathe. My lungs are going to explode. Almost as if I'm underwater.

Like he was.

He turns. There's a knife. Someone slashes at him. A red gash opens on his forearm and he drops the pole. Slash again, and he dives out of the way. Into the water. The water is greenish-black from the shade trees above. He surfaces, but the water is too deep, much too deep for him to reach the bottom. He struggles to stay afloat, to find something to grab onto, but in his panic everything falls through his grasp, until the only thing left is the sound of splashing mingling with laughter.

"He can't go fishing!" I shout, finally getting the air into my lungs. I gasp, again and again and again.

Justin turns to me, his eyes orange with firelight. "You've heard this one before?"

I can't stop shaking. "Please, Justin. Can we just go to bed? I'm tired. *Please.*"

He studies me. "All right. It's late anyway. We have to get up early."

It's only then I realize Angela and Hugo are both staring at me. Ange says, "You look tired, Ki." But I know from her expression she means I look a lot worse than tired. I hug myself tight, creeping closer to the fire, but even that doesn't stop the shivers. Ange whispers to Justin, "You'll have to tell me the rest later."

But I know the rest. Somehow, I was there. I saw it all.

And I saw him die.

CHAPTER FOUR

I curl up on the shag throw rug in the dark bathroom, which is lit only by moonlight streaming through the window. I press my fists to my eyes until I see fireworks. Down here, I don't hear the rush of the water. Down here, I almost feel safe.

My dad is a teacher at my high school. He teaches my European History class and about fifteen extracurricular activities, from Driver's Ed to Debate Club. The parents of freshmen learning how to drive don't have to worry about a thing, really; besides Justin, my dad is probably the safest person in the state of Maine. I mean, I had to beg and plead with him, nonstop, for three months, just to get him to agree to a weekend camping trip two hours from home. And when he finally agreed, he handed me a copy of *Camping for Dummies* and quizzed me on each chapter, every Saturday. In fact, should we run out of the twelve days' worth of food he packed for me before I left, I know how to set a pencil snare so I can catch a rabbit.

Justin is on the swim team at school. When my dad noticed that we were hanging out a lot more in the hallways, he got that worried look in his eye, but he never said anything. And one day I went to Justin's swim practice to cheer him on from the bleachers, and Justin came up to me between laps to say hi. He was usually very suave, because this was the beginning of our relationship and he was trying to present that really good side of himself that everyone puts forward when relationships are new. But right then, he was nervous. "How are you?" he asked, fidgeting.

"Fine. Are you worried about the meet coming up?" I asked him.

He shook his head, water spraying on my lap.

"Nervous about . . . um, me being here?" I ventured. Maybe my presence intimidated him and would affect his performance.

"No, that's not it. I'm fine," he said. I could tell he was distracted. He kept looking past me, toward the back of the bleachers.

So I stayed for a little while longer, wondering if he was just not interested anymore. Which made my stomach drop, because for weeks I'd thought about him more than I breathed. Then, as he hurried back to the pool, I got up and started to leave. And who did I see at the top of the bleachers, his nose buried in *The Establishment of European Hegemony 1415–1715*?

"Dad," I said to him later, "I'm fifteen. I don't need you following me everywhere I go. And Justin is a good guy."

He'd had a strange, sad smile on his face. "I know, I know," he said.

My stomach did cartwheels. Nobody could doubt that Justin was the most upstanding of guys. Good grades, always deflected trouble, made friends easily with everyone. If my dad had a problem with him, then I was positive there was *nobody* in school he'd approve of. Maybe nobody in the *world*. "Well, what don't you like about him?" I asked.

He didn't answer, and I was glad, because I thought I knew. It was such an embarrassing thing, I really didn't want to hear him say it. He couldn't cope with me growing up, I was his little girl, his everything, and no guy would ever be good enough for his "everything." I guess I couldn't blame him, but at the same time I imagined myself sitting home, alone, at the age of sixty-two, still not allowed to date.

From then on, I'd often catch him in the hallways outside the pool when I went to watch Justin at swim practice. I'd just see a shadow, a hint of his army-green herringbone blazer, a flash of his scruffy beard in the doorway. It was almost as if I'd drawn a line in the doorway and he'd made the decision not to pass it. But he couldn't stop himself from checking up on me from afar.

I didn't mention it to him. I thought I understood. I didn't realize how wrong I was.

One day, I went to watch Justin practice golf. Justin isn't a great golfer, but he wants to be one, so he joined the team. That first day, I looked around and around the field and my dad was nowhere to be seen. *What about watching Justin golf is so safe?* I thought. *Or what about watching Justin swim is so dangerous? He thinks I'd be so enamored of Justin in a Speedo I'd jump him?*

But suddenly it came to me. My dad wasn't having trouble coping with me growing up. He didn't have a problem with Justin at all. What he had a problem with was *the thought of me drowning, like she did.* Even the thought of a swimming pool. Suddenly it hit me, why I hadn't been to the beach in ages, why there was no water anywhere near our house, why, when I was invited to pool parties, he always made sure we were busy. It was crazy, but it was true. He was that freaked out by my mom's death that he couldn't stand it. But me, on the other hand . . . I was fine with it. In fact, it didn't bother me at all.

I decided to confront him. I knew exactly how. "Dad, I'm thinking of taking swimming classes," I told him casually after our usual mac-and-cheese dinner.

His eyes filled with dread. For a moment he looked like he might choke on his mouthful, but he brought his napkin to his mouth, wiped his graying beard, and cleared his throat thoughtfully. "You're not a strong swimmer, Ki."

That was true. I hadn't been swimming since before mom died. "Well, duh, that's why I want to take classes," I said. "Justin said he'd help me practice."

"You have yearbook and band. Doesn't it interfere—"

"Nope. It's good. I checked already."

He shook his head. "I think you need to keep up with your studies. It's just too much."

"Dad," I said, the anger boiling in me. "It's. A. Pool. It's not some raging river. And what happened to her will never happen to me! Stop constantly trying to protect me from her!"

He'd stared at me for a while, silently, gripping his paper napkin until it ripped down the center. And then he got up from the table, from his half-eaten dinner, and walked into his bedroom without another word. We didn't talk for days after that, and when we finally did, it was like the previous conversation had never happened. But I was still angry. Really, how could he be so ridiculous? To what lengths would he go? Maybe next he would forbid me from taking baths. Walking in rain showers. Getting Big Gulps at the 7-E.

But now I can't help but wonder if there was something more to his concern. I'd never told him about the visions I'd had. It seems crazy to think that just because my mom drowned in a river, he'd want to keep me completely isolated from water. And yet he's been almost fanatical about it. He'd yanked me away from the river back home so quickly, we didn't even have time to pack. And now, why am I having visions, visions I haven't had in ten years, now that I'm by the water again? *Maybe there is something else he's afraid of.*

No. What else could there be? He was just being protective. I'm his little girl, after all.

I stand up and twist the handles on the faucet, hoping to splash some water on my face, but nothing happens. Then I remember that the water has been turned off. Perfect.

It's just my overactive imagination, I tell myself. *Those things I saw . . . they're not real. They can't hurt me.*

Someone raps on the door. "Ki? You okay?" Justin.

"Fine," I say, wiping my face with some wadded-up toilet paper, not that it's doing much good. "I'm just—" I stop, wondering what I can lie about, considering there's no water in here. "I'm good."

I click open the door slowly and find his concerned eyes in the darkness. "You sure?"

"Oh. Yeah."

"Have to be up early tomorrow. The sunrise from the top of Grey Mountain is amazing. Want to go for a hike when we wake up?"

Sure. Trekking through the predawn blackness in freezing temperatures. Sounds lovely. I don't say anything, but my body stiffens.

"It's okay. Maybe I'll go myself, then," he says, putting his arm around me. "Nice and warm in here. Why don't you sleep in a bed tonight?"

"I told you, I'm *fine,*" I say, but it comes out more like a snarl. I'm going to be perfectly okay here, and nobody—not him, not my dad—is going to tell me any different. I muster a smile. "Lead the way. Out to the campsite. Bring it on."

He must be fooled by my resolve, because he throws up his hands. "All right. Yes, sir!" he replies, saluting.

We go back to our sleeping bags. Hugo is already snoring, making this embarrassingly loud noise that will scare anything away, so we don't need to worry about wild animals raiding our camp in the middle of the night. Not that I'm expecting to sleep much. Angela is sitting propped up on her elbows, looking at me across the fire. "You okay, Honey Bunches of Oats?" she asks me.

For as long as I can remember, Angela and I have been calling each other by the names of popular breakfast cereals. "Sure thing, Cocoa Puffs," I answer, pulling back the cover of my bag and inspecting it for creepy-crawlies.

"I can get you a cold compress or something." Her eyes are big and round again, worried. It's amazing how like her mother she is. The minute I arrived in Maine, Aunt Missy was at my side, playing Florence Nightingale. She was the Cold Compress Queen, always bringing something to put on my forehead and massaging my temples until I'd relax.

"I'm good," I say, smiling at her, though my head is throbbing and I'd love someone to massage my temples. It makes me think of my mother's headaches.

No. I'm not like her.

When I slide into the bag, I still don't feel warm. I move closer to Justin but I don't think it will do any good, even when he drapes his big arm around me and pulls me to his chest. I close my eyes, concentrating on the crackle of the fire, and slip my clammy hand into Justin's warm one. But the only thing I can hear now is the river. It whirrs along, until soon my hand in Justin's doesn't feel just clammy . . . it feels wet. My feet, too.

I move my legs, but it's like wading against a tide. They ache. My feet are submerged in water—icy, numbing water. I can hear them sloshing through it as I move them in the bag.

What the—

I jump upright and kick off the sleeping bag. My wool socks are completely dry. Justin has his eyes closed and is lazily feeling around for me, to pull me back. "Um, I thought I felt a spider," I whisper, but he doesn't seem interested in the explanation, just mumbles a good night. I go back to the place Justin's body has carved out for me, and hope hope hope that I'll be able to get even an hour's worth of sleep tonight.

Justin's breathing becomes deep and soft, lulling me. His breath on my ear drowns out the whispers of the river. Sleep comes.

CHAPTER FIVE

I'm woken as a trickle of water slides down my cheek. Wet, again. I try to push the thought away. *It's just my imagination, my stupid imagination,* I think, when another droplet lands on my forehead.

Water?

I turn onto my side, stretching, reaching for the clock at my bedside, but my fingers wrap around something wet, cold, and stringy. Weird. I roll back over, wipe my eyes with the heels of my hands, and try to open them. Instead of that helping me to see, my retinas start to burn. I keep blinking. Again and again, until I focus on my palms. They're smeared with black mud, bits of gravel, and slivers of grass.

Springing upright, I remember. I'm outside, camping. I'm in another world, so different from my bedroom. There's a thick mist hugging the trees, only a peek of their dark trunks exposed. A thin drizzle is falling. I blink, finally focusing on Hugo, who is yawning and stoking the dying fire. He looks haggard, every bit like he just spent the last six hours sleeping on the cold, hard ground.

Then I remember the night before. The storytelling around the fire. And I realize something.

I slept. I slept well, in fact. Really well. So well that I forgot where I was. Considering all the weird things that happened yesterday, and what lies ahead, that's nothing short of amazing.

I look around for Justin, but it's just Hugo and me. No Angela, either. The wind has picked up; it's whistling through the trees, carrying the sound of the rushing river. "Where is everyone?"

"Went for a morning hike. To see the sunrise. Or something twisted like that." He clears his throat. "I need coffee. You want?"

"Yeah," I say, rubbing the sleep from my eyes. "Why didn't you go?"

He fixes the pot over the fire and leans back. "Saving my energy for the river. Besides, I didn't want you to wake up to a bear crapping on your head."

I can't believe I missed all the commotion of them getting up and leaving. I was sleeping *that* soundly. What a difference a good night's sleep can make. Rafting doesn't seem quite so scary now. But hiking up a mountain at the crack of dawn to see the sun? Crazy. I guess Angela and Justin are two peas in a pod that way. A feeling of dread passes over me as I realize something. They went to see the *sunrise*. "But it's raining."

"Just started. It was dark an hour ago," he answers. "When they left. To see the sun come up, it helps to leave before it actually *comes up.*"

What a snot. I guess there are some things a good night's sleep will never remedy.

"But . . ." I stand there, trying to think of something to say about the two of them running off together on a rainy day to see the sunrise that won't make me look like a jealous girl-friend, but everything seems wrong. Really, I'm not worried. It isn't possible for him to do anything underhanded. Even thinking about it would give him hives. And Angela—not only is she my cousin, she's like Mother Teresa. They're so . . . alike.

Hugo picks up his camera and grins. "I got some good pictures. You know you were drooling?"

My mouth drops open, and all of a sudden I can feel a spot of drool hanging over my bottom lip. I swipe at it. "If I find out you took pictures of me while I was sleeping, that thing is going to be in the river faster than you can—"

"Hey, hey, hey. Chill," he says, as if he wasn't the one who started it. "I only photograph subjects that interest me."

I glare at him. That's it. Angela is no longer my cousin. It's bad enough I have to deal with his attitude every day after school in the yearbook office, but this is torture. There are still a few weeks left before yearbooks get printed. I've been toying with the idea all year long since I was appointed editor of the seniors section, but now I've pretty much decided that the entry under his graduation picture is going to have an unfortunate typo: "Huge A. Holbrook." A smile comes to my lips as I imagine it. "When do we have to leave?"

"Right about now," Justin's voice echoes somewhere in the woods. A second later, he's climbing down the rocky slope toward us, wearing a yellow hooded rain jacket, hiking boots, and shorts despite the frigid weather.

Angela follows behind him, hands in her pockets. "Well, that was a big bust." She sighs, annoyed. "Maybe tomorrow."

"Come on. We've got to be there by eight." Justin starts stuffing his backpack with supplies. Suddenly he looks at me and leans forward, kissing my forehead. "Morning. Sleep well?"

"Yep. Great," I say.

"You ready to do some rafting?" I'm about to nod and say "Ready as I'll ever be" when he narrows his eyes at me. "Going for the tribal warrior look?"

"Why?" I begin, and then I realize he's staring at my cheeks. Out of the corner of my vision, I can see something black on my nose. Dirt. I start to swipe at it with my hand and Justin takes his sleeve and wipes it, too. Feeling stupid, I ask, "Better?"

He nods. "I kind of liked it the other way, though. Made you look tough."

He would. That's Justin for you. He'd much rather a girl sport war paint than lip gloss.

Northeast Outfitters is right across Route 201, so once we pack up all our stuff, we head across the road and into a log cabin. There are already groups of people hanging around outside on the deck, wearing wet suits and slurping down coffees in Styrofoam cups. Most of them are older people, in their thirties and forties, maybe. They look really adventurous. Well, more adventurous than I do, I'm sure. Hell, I'm nervous about how stupid I'm going to look in my rented wet suit.

Here we're close enough to the river that I can look across to the other bank. Scattered among the black pines are bits of gray stone and concrete, what looks like the broken remains of some old building. For a moment I think I see someone moving there, but when I focus I realize it must only be the pine trees sweeping back and forth in the wind. At least, I hope.

When we go inside, Justin saunters up to the desk, self-assured. "Hey, Spiffy!" he calls, and I know he's talking to Pat Skiffington, one of the guys who work here and one of Justin's oldest friends. Justin's family has been coming to the Outfitters for so long that the two families exchange Christmas cards—the last one I saw from the Skiffingtons had Frosty careening down a river in a yellow raft. Even when planning for this trip was in the earliest stages, it was always "Spiffy will hook us up" and "Spiffy knows this river better than anyone." I peer around the shoulders of the other people in the room to see a guy with the most shocking red hair and freckles clap Justin on the back and say, "Yo, man!" He's wearing a Red Sox cap turned backward and a rumpled T-shirt, and he looks about as unspiffy as a person can get.

I hang back with Angela, who is trying to find one of her

booties in her bag. She and Justin brought their own wet suits, since they're up here all the time, and Hugo borrowed his brother's. But for me, it's rental city. Ugh. I don't really like the idea of a suit that hugged someone else's most private body parts hugging mine, but I'm determined not to complain. I'm determined to be okay with roughing it, which was why I pretended it was *just fine* that we didn't brush our teeth, despite the thick film on mine that I keep trying to wipe away with my tongue. I bite my lip and focus on the pictures in a glass case along with a huge map of the state. Photographs of dozens of smiling people in ballpark-mustard-color rafts, surrounded by white water. They all look so happy. I don't know if it's possible for me to smile like that. Well, not surrounded by a raging river, at least.

Then I turn to another picture that looks out of place among all the color photos. It's faded and yellowing, part of an old newspaper article, and the frame itself is cracked and covered with what looks like years of dust. The headline on it says: RIDE THE DEAD RIVER WITH THE SKIFFINGTON BROTHERS. There are two men, one clean-shaven in a suit and tie, and the other in a beard and a flannel shirt, standing under a GRAND OPENING sign on the porch of what must be the same cabin I'm standing in. The date on it is July 18, 1992.

"Got it!" Angela says, triumphant, hopping around to squeeze the bootie onto her foot. She's already wearing her wet suit. It's cute, mostly black with a little pink stitching. She looks even better in the wet suit than she does in regular clothes: strong, statuesque, and athletic. I think I will probably look like a full garbage bag in mine: lumpy, shapeless, and sadly waiting to go to where its life will end.

Justin motions to us. I move through the crowd and lean against the desk as he hands me a pen. "You guys just need to sign this release," he says.

I read it as both Hugo and Angela hurriedly scribble their names on the line. I have to focus on my breathing when I go down the list of possible risks: "disease, strains, fractures, partial and/or total paralysis, death, or other ailments that cause serious disability."

I repeat Angela's words to calm myself. *Smooth sailing.*

Then I stop when I see: "Signature of parent or guardian if under 18." I look at Justin. He mouths, *It's okay. Just do it.*

I hesitate for only a second. This is Justin. Justin, who always checks my seat belt to make sure it's fastened before he takes Monster out. Justin, who religiously stays to my left when we're walking down the sidewalk, to protect me from whatever peril might lie in the street. He wouldn't have me sign anything unless there really was no danger involved. It'll just be a leisurely jaunt down the river. *Smooth sailing.* I grab the pen and sign *Kiandra Levesque.*

"Let's get you a suit. It's twenty to rent," Spiffy says, inspecting me as I fork over the crumpled bill that's been glued with sweat to my palm. I think he's probably just trying to figure out what size I am, but when he turns around and walks into the back of the office, Justin winks at me.

"He does *not* want me," I mutter.

"Totally does."

"You're crazy."

"I'm right."

I stick my tongue out at him just as Spiffy appears in the doorway with an amorphous gray thing with pee-yellow arms that looks like it has seen better days. "You can try it on here," he tells me, motioning to the back. "Want some help?"

I look at Justin helplessly. Is that some backwoods pickup line?

He grins at me. "Let him help you get dressed," he whispers. "It will be the highlight of his young life."

I scowl at him as Spiffy just pulls aside the curtain and lets me pass, as if he's dressed teenage girls in neoprene a million times before. "You wearing long underwear?"

The curtain swings back, effectively shielding me from Justin's *I told you so* expression. I nod, stripping off my North Face jacket. I'm actually wearing two layers of water-resistant skin and two pairs of extra-thick wool socks that go up to my knees because I know I'll be freezing. Justin is wearing long underwear, and if he, the Snowman himself, the man who is known to traipse around in the dead of winter in nothing but gym shorts, is wearing long underwear on this trip, I know we're talking about some *serious* cold. I stare at the suit as Spiffy holds it out to me. "How do I get it on?" I laugh nervously. "I've never—"

"Here," he says, leaning over and helping me step into it. I nearly fall over a few times before zipping it up over my long underwear. As I'm leaning over to fasten the booties, feeling as flexible as a sausage in its casing, I realize the suit smells like feet. Feet with a thin Febreze mask.

I swallow as I look at myself in a floor-to-ceiling mirror. I'm pretty thin, but that doesn't matter: I *look* like a sausage, or rather like a plastic bag of potatoes, lumpy and round. "Um, so," I say, trying to take the focus off my foxy wet-suit-clad body, "your dad started the Outfitters?"

He nods. "My dad and his twin brother."

"Twin? I was looking at the picture in the lobby. They don't look very alike."

"They aren't. They lead completely different lives. My uncle is really into rafting and convinced my dad to invest in the Outfitters. My dad isn't into that stuff at all, but he has a lot of capital." He smiles. "My dad kind of hates this place now. He goes where the money is, and this is pretty much a money suck. I think that picture out front is the only one I have of the two of them together." He holds out a plate of assorted breakfast goodies. "Pastry?"

I pluck a blueberry muffin off the plate. "Don't they like each other?"

He shrugs. "Not even close. They may be twins, but Uncle Robert is so different. A free spirit. He was never around much, even after the Outfitters was started. Then he left two years ago to hike the Appalachian Trail and we haven't heard from him since. But the guy always does things like that. Crazy things. My dad doesn't know the first thing about rafting, so I pretty much run this place. I've been down the Dead a thousand times. Your boyfriend is one of my best customers. And your cousin. They talk about you all the time."

"They do?" I blurt, almost spitting out a bit of my muffin. I can't imagine what they would say, other than *She's not exactly an outdoorsy girl.*

He checks a clock on the wall and says, "We'd better get you out there. Bus leaves in five."

"Okay. Are you going to be on our raft?" I ask. Maybe having The Guy Who Knows Everything About the Dead on my raft would stop my stomach from clenching like it is.

He shakes his head. "There's a group of novices going out, and they'll need my help more than you. With Justin and Angela, you're in good hands. Your guide is Michael. He's a good guy. Been with us a couple years."

"Oh," I say, unable to hide my disappointment. "Is it really wild out there?"

I'm hoping he'll tell me that no, it's calm, for some reason they just can't understand. You can see your reflection in the water. Babies can bathe in it. Instead, he says, "Oh yeah. Wildest of the year is right now. Over seven thousand see-eff-esses."

"See what?"

"Cubic feet per second. Great time to come up. Great time."

I gulp. Oh yeah. *Great* time.

I feel all stiff in this getup; bending my limbs is nearly impossible. When I walk, I'm sure I look like I just peed my pants. We step out to the front and I see through the picture window that a bunch of the rafters are already boarding the white school bus that's going to take us to put-in.

We're all alone in the building, so when I hear someone behind me breathe *What the devil is that?* I turn back to Spiffy and try to figure out what he's talking about. But he's just looking at me blankly.

"What the devil is *what?*" I ask, confused.

He stares at me.

"You just said—"

"I didn't say anything." He's staring at me as if I have a horn protruding from my forehead. Come to think of it, it didn't sound much like his voice. It had a rougher edge to it, but not only that, there was an accent. Australian, I think. I turn back to where the voice came from, but the room is empty. All I see is that picture of the two Skiffington brothers, smiling together.

"Um, okay," I say, and then try to cover up by saying, "So, what's over on the other side of the river?"

He waves his hand over there. "Oh, death. Destruction. All that good stuff." I guess I must be staring at him, because he says, "I'm kidding. Well, only partly. It's an old cemetery."

Ah. Perfect.

He continues, "Haven't you ever heard of what the west bank means?"

I shake my head.

"Many civilizations used to believe the east bank of a river symbolized birth and renewal. The west bank symbolized death. And so people lived on the east bank. They buried their dead on the west bank."

I shudder. We really should not be talking about death at a time like this. I'm about to say something like "How interesting," although really I wish he'd talk about bunnies and rainbows, when it comes again:

What the devil is that?

This time I'm sure of it. It came from the direction of the picture. I stall in the doorway and turn to Spiffy right away, but he's just jingling his keys and trying to usher me out the door so he can lock up the office. I want to ask him, "You didn't hear that?" but I already know the answer. He didn't hear a thing.

Maybe it was just the wind whistling through the trees outside.

But when I climb down the stairs to the gravel driveway, the first thing I notice is that the pines surrounding the Outfitters cabin are completely still. Overhead, a blackbird caws. We may be on the living side of the river, but I can't stop myself from shivering as I board the bus and we rumble down the dirt road toward the put-in site.

CHAPTER SIX

Justin holds my hand on the bus ride down to the river. He likes to trace letters in my palm, secret messages, but this time I'm only getting fragments. First a *U*, then some other letter, then a *K*. He looks at me expectantly, but I'm just puzzled.

He does it again. This time I concentrate on it. *U O K. You okay?*

I smile at him and nod, even though my hands are shaking. For some reason, I can't stop myself from looking at the Death side of the river. It probably doesn't look much different from this side, but I can't get it out of my head. And if I was going to start making up voices in my head, why would my head choose a phrase like *What the devil is that?* And in the accent of a gruff Australian guy? I never knew my subconscious was that creative.

The bus bumps along, and the blueberry muffin I'd taken nibbles of in the back of the office bumps along with it in my stomach, threatening to make an escape. Hugo is mumbling something about how the zipper on his wet suit is chafing his neck, and meanwhile Angela, looking prettier than I've ever seen her, is just staring out the window at the river like it's a cookie she wants to take a big bite of. Justin is tracing messages on my hand again, but this time all I catch is a *V* and a *U*. It doesn't matter. I know what he's saying. I turn his palm over and trace *LUV U 2* on his.

The bus jostles us along for a few miles and then turns toward the river, down a narrow path that's more potholes than road. A beefy guy with a crew cut, probably in his mid-twenties, comes down the aisle, finally stopping at the seat in front of us. "Hey, I'm Michael. Your guide," he says to us, shaking Justin's hand. "Not that you'll need a guide."

"Have you been out there on this release yet?" Justin asks.

Michael exhales. "Oh yeah. Yesterday. It's going to be a blast. Great time."

Justin and Angela nod, excited. I look out the window to see rows of equipment lined up in metal cages near a long pier. I guess we're here, at put-in. Everyone starts funneling off of the bus and for a moment I can't seem to find my legs, but then I stand and follow Justin and the rest of my group. Someone hands me a paddle and straps a helmet and life jacket on me and we walk out toward the pier. We wait for the other groups of people to load onto their rafts and push off, and then it's our turn. I can't believe I'm finally doing this. I step into the raft and it bucks and I look for a seat. A seat belt. Something so I won't fall out.

"Where do we sit?" I ask Justin.

He pats the edge of the raft.

"But there's—that's—impossible," I stammer. It all looks so precarious, like dangling one's feet out the window of a high-rise building. And he knows I have no sense of balance. I sometimes fall over walking on level ground. This is just an accident waiting to happen.

Justin knocks on my helmet lightly. "You'll be fine. I'll be right behind you."

I swallow and attempt to sit down on the raft, then straighten again. This can't be right. I'll fall out the second the raft moves. "Wait. Where do I put my feet? Do I, um, straddle it?"

Angela laughs and sits like she's slipping into a comfy recliner. "No. Keep your legs in. Like this."

I follow her, but I might as well be sitting on a marshmallow. The raft pitches a little, then a lot when Justin sits down. I lurch forward, then dig the heels of my water shoes in and steady myself before I can kiss Michael's backside. He's sitting in front of me, so I'm flanked by two burly, manly men. Nothing to worry about, right?

Wrong.

Michael strokes his scruffy goatee and smiles at me. "Virgin?"

"Um, excuse me?"

"First time on the river?"

"Oh, er. Yes," I say, thinking, *Does he even need to ask that?*

"Don't worry. Piece of cake," he says, but I can't help feeling that everyone is saying that only because they're a lot braver than I am. If it's a piece of cake, why am I wearing a helmet that makes my head look twice its normal size? "Now, my first time as guide. Two years ago. That was a story."

"Oh really?" I mutter, not wanting to hear, since with my luck it probably has to do with someone's death or dismemberment. I look over the edge of the raft at the dark water frothing beneath me, and I try to take deep, cleansing breaths. *If only my dad could see me now. He'd be so . . . out of control.*

I picture my dad's face, turning tomato-red under his beard, his eyes bulging as he condemns me to spending the summer at home, grounded. And for what? This *totally fun experience?* We haven't even pushed off yet, and I already feel seasick. Maybe Dad was right.

Michael obviously doesn't sense my lack of enthusiasm in reliving his exciting first days on the river, because he continues on: "Yeah. One of the factories upriver, on the Androscoggin, made clothing forms. You know, mannequins and stuff. It closed down in the 1950s. But two years ago they were demolishing all the factories to make way for some condos. And somehow a bunch of the forms ended up in the river, and during the dam release, with the water churning the way it was, they looked like dead bodies."

Of course, dead bodies had to be in there somewhere. But it is kind of interesting. I find myself saying "Really?" and wanting to hear more.

"Yeah. Funny thing was, all the guides were jumping in to save them. So we were soaked before we even started. And it's not fun to spend three hours soaked on this river in early

May." He laughs. "The good thing was, I've never had it any worse than that first time."

Well, that's a good sign, at least. Surprisingly, I feel a bit of calm trickle over me.

"Okay, Chief," Justin says from the back. For some reason he calls guys in a position of authority Chief; I guess it's in preparation for his police job. Either that or he likes to pretend he's part of an Indian tribe. "We're all set."

The calm doesn't last; my heart buckles in my chest as we push off. For a second I look longingly at the pier, but only for a second, because soon we're in the middle of the river. No turning back. I grip the paddle in my hand so hard that I'm surprised my fingers don't make dents in the handle. I'm so stiff, afraid to even breathe because that might throw my balance off.

After a few minutes, I loosen up a little and exhale. I manage to take my eyes off the river ahead for a moment or two to take in the shimmery, light green buds appearing on the trees and enjoy the fresh, clean smell of new spring growth. *Actually, it's not bad. Just coasting,* I tell myself. *Great scenery.* We dip and toss, but only gently. Michael leans his oar over the side and begins paddling, so I do, too, imitating him perfectly. I almost forget that there are rapids up ahead, until Michael calls out, "Spencer Rips is first."

"Spencer who?" I ask, but then I see it. Peaks of white on the river ahead. At one point, the rushing water seems to disappear into a void, only to show up farther downstream. *A waterfall.* I want to hide at the center of the raft, but instead, I follow Michael and just brace myself as we dip into the wave. A wall of icy water hits me square in the face and I bite my lip, tasting grit. Angela lets out a shriek—not of fear, knowing her. And I'm right, because two seconds later she shouts, "Awesome!" I swallow, thinking that this is how different my cousin is from me; never in my life could I consider eating dirt to be awesome. I don't think my paddling does much, but I keep doing it, because everyone else is, and what if it's all that's keeping me from an icy swim in the Dead?

A few tense minutes later, the river evens out. I exhale slowly and Michael looks back, smiling. "No sweat, right?"

Justin claps me on the back. "You did it."

I did it. Yes!

Michael relaxes and says, "So, as I was saying, this job is crazy. That was the first of many, shall we say, *interesting* excursions on the Dead."

Now I'm all ears. Almost relaxed, even. "Like what?"

"Well, there were the dudes who insisted on rafting completely naked, except for their helmets and paddling jackets. And the ladies who were part of a reality TV show. They thought it was a sightseeing tour of the river. One of them chipped a nail and all hell broke loose."

I laugh.

"Yeah. Robert was all like, 'Put a sock in it and get your arses on the raft.' And he took out a knife and started waving it at them."

"Robert?" I ask. "You mean Robert Skiffington? Pat's uncle?"

"Yeah. He's crazy. He used to jump into the river in the winter without a wet suit. And after the ride, he'd run around base camp screaming and laughing and peeking in the tents of the female campers." He laughs. "The Australian outback must have fried his brains, man."

I stare at him for a second. Something clicks in my mind. "Robert Skiffington was Australian?"

"Well, no. He was born here. But he lived there awhile or something." He laughs. "Man, I miss him. We keep wondering when he's coming back."

Somehow, even though a thin drizzle is still falling, I see the early light of dawn poking through the trees behind the Outfitters office building. I see a wiry man, setting off with hiking boots and a backpack that is half his size slung behind him. I see him stop to gaze out on the river as the shadows of the trees stretch in the new pink-orange light. His eyes mist over. *Well, I'm not going to be seeing you, my dear, for a while.*

And then, not a moment later,

What the devil is that?

And suddenly I know something, almost as sure as I know my own name. I know that two years ago, Robert Skiffington left with his pack, hiking up toward the Appalachian Trail. I know that he saw a cold white hand protruding from the water in the shadows of the dawn. I know that he said *What the devil is that?* before sliding down the embankment, his head thudding against a log with a sickly crack as his hand reached for that white limb, only to find the solid, completely inhuman material of a mannequin form, before he faded out of consciousness.

And I know he's not coming back. Because the truth is, he never left.

CHAPTER SEVEN

O*kay*, I tell myself. *Breathe.*

This has got to be my imagination. Robert Skiffington is very much alive, hiking the Appalachian Trail somewhere miles away from here.

Isn't he?

I exhale as the vision subsides, but my eyes immediately dart to the side, to something I know does not belong. There, sitting where Angela should be, and wearing a prim white gown, is Lannie. She smiles through her tears. "Remember me, Tootsie?"

At first I'm surprised I know her name, know anything at all about her, but then it all comes flooding back to me. She was one of my friends, one of my constant visions when I lived on the Delaware. She was always there with me, telling me stories about the summers she and her sister spent on the water. They'd go tubing and have picnics by the river, and it all seemed like so much fun. Lannie was the daring one, jumping into the river without a second thought, laughing endlessly at me whenever I tried to take things slow. I always wished she was my sister, because there were no other children where I lived and I desperately wanted other kids to play with. She was my one and only friend. My *imaginary* friend.

"You're not—Why are you—" I sputter, and then all at once she disappears and is replaced by that girl in the pink party dress, her eyes dark and hopeless.

I'm snapped back to reality before she can open her mouth and spew mud. The waves churn around the raft, matching the tumult going on inside me. "What are you doing here?" I ask her, but by that time, she's gone.

Crack. I hear it again and again, that sickening sound of Robert's skull smashing against a rock or a log or whatever. Always *What the devil is that?* followed a minute later by that horrifying sound that can only mean the end of Robert Skiffington's life. He's dead. Gone.

And somehow, I'm the only one in the world who knows it.

The whispers start. At first I think it's nothing, the new spring leaves rustling gently around us. But eventually I can make out actual words. So many different voices, speaking at once. *Asked . . . devil . . . you . . .* A whirl of words, nonsensical ramblings, growing louder and louder, until they drown out all other sounds. Pain blooms in my forehead and doesn't subside when I press my hand against my temple. Instead, the voices only grow stronger. Now I can almost make them out. I know that if they get any louder, my head is bound to explode.

I turn around, still clutching the paddle. "Justin," I whisper, trying to catch my breath. Somehow, though we're in the outdoors, it feels like there are walls closing in on me. Walls of water, bearing down on me, waiting to sweep me downriver. Justin is only an arm's length behind me, and yet it seems like he's a mile away. "I need to get out."

I can tell from the look in his eyes that he's hoping I'm kidding, because I know there's no way I can simply get out. Instinctively he moves forward and puts a hand on my shoulder. "What? What's wrong?"

By now the voices are screaming in my head.

I did everything you asked of me.

"I can't—" I swallow. "I can't breathe."

He's the one. Get him.

Justin scuttles to my side, grabbing the paddle from me. "Calm down," he says. "You're okay." But I'm not. My heartbeat is thudding in my head. My mind, my ears, my entire body is pulsating, filled with echoes. Echoes of the dead.

The girl in the pink party dress, filth spurting from the open crevasse of her mouth, reaches for me first. I squeeze my eyes shut, but I see them all perfectly in the darkness. When I force my eyes open, everything is swirling. Masses of pine needles look like matted human hair, and branches like brittle brown bones, churning in white foam. And then suddenly, from the foam, I see the hands. Ghostly fingers reaching up, sliding along the edge of the raft. Reaching for me.

"Oh my God," I manage. Is this what my mother saw before she . . . Suddenly I'm screaming. Angela's now looking

71

at me, launching into Florence Nightingale mode. I hear her voice among the others, distorted like a record being played at too slow a speed, *What's wrong? Ki, what's wrong?* But the only thing I can get out is "Justin" as I claw at him, grasping for him desperately.

He's like an image in a dream I keep running to, though every step closer brings me one step away. Though his arms are around me, they're not keeping me safe. It's almost like they're pushing me toward the waves, too. I try to wrench myself free and move to the center of the raft, but everything is forcing me toward the water. Or maybe it's just that the river is pulling me to it, wanting to hold me closer. Another wave kicks up and splashes us, jerking the raft to the side. We're in another rapids, and suddenly I'm over the edge and Justin is holding me by the arms. My body is in the water, and, strangely, it's not bitingly cold. It feels warm, almost inviting, but I still clutch for something to get me out. Michael reaches over the side, trying to pull me back, shouting, "Hold on! Hold on!" Someone calls, "What the hell is going on?" I can tell that nobody knows what's happening. I feel the pressure on my legs, under the water. As strong as Justin and Michael are, they're no match for the hands that are under the water, clutching me. Pulling me down.

"Don't let me go," I whimper to Justin, and he strains to say "I won't," but I can tell he's confused, unsure as to why he can't hoist me back into the raft. I weigh half of what he does. He obviously can't see what I can feel. The dozens of hands on my legs and waist, pulling me down until I can't fight anymore. Slowly I let go and take one last, strangled breath before sliding under the surface.

It's strange: once the water wraps around me, even the rush of it around me sounds like only one word, being whispered in my ear over and over again. *Welcome.*

I'm drowning.

In my head, I'm screaming. It feels as though I've been launched through a pinball machine. Like my body is careening at breakneck speed, being tossed every which way, and I have no control. I try to move my arms in another direction but I'm beaten into submission by a force much more powerful than me. Something jams against my cheek, pushing my head back so far that the bones of my neck grate against one another. I try to force it away, flailing my arms wildly, but then I hit against another hard thing. Everything is rocketing in only one direction, and I have no idea what lies at the very end. I don't think I'll find out. I know that before I reach the end, I'll be dead.

My lungs are beating against my chest, exploding. My heart thuds in my ears. I look up, toward the ripples of sunlight. They're just a blur now, because I'm moving too fast. I need to get there. Somehow. I reach my hand out, but instead of propelling myself upward, all I do is bring back a handful of soft, mucky stuff, like a tangled mane of hair. Like my mother's hair. I make another attempt to scramble upward but I find myself just sinking deeper, and the lights above begin to fade with the burning sensation in my lungs.

The last thing that enters my mind is that it's funny how we try so hard not to be like our parents, because that never works out. I'm going to die here, in a river. Just like her.

CHAPTER EIGHT

First there are the whispers.

I did . . .

What the . . .

That's the . . .

I keep still, listening, but the words never come together to make sense. They're just words, as if read from a dictionary, phrases that never mean anything. The morning's biting cold stings my cheeks. I'm still wearing that impossibly uncomfortable wet suit, but instead of being near-frozen, I'm sweating underneath the layers of wool clothes. I open my eyes, and all I see is the gray, sad sky and black, bare branches above me. A large crow glides overhead, cawing ominously.

I'm alive. Amazingly. I must be. If I were dead, my head wouldn't hurt as much, would it?

I sit up. As I do, my head throbs, begging me to rest, but I push against gravity and straighten. When I'm erect, my hair whips over my eyes. I pull it back, but it's slimy in places, gritty in others, and knotted like seaweed. Where is my helmet?

The whispering continues, which is odd because I'm alone. But then it changes somehow—was it not whispering but the sound of rushing water? I look around. Water moving everywhere, all around me. *No, no, not more water!* I want to retch at the sight of it. When I swallow, there's something thick and gritty in the back of my throat. The water laps at my toes, almost as if it's trying to touch them, to grab me and pull me back toward it. I'm sitting on a small island right in the middle of the river.

I scan the horizon for cheerful yellow rafts. When we set off, there were dozens. Now I can't see a one. I search the riverbanks to either side of me, but the only witnesses to my peril are tall pines, bowing to me in the stiff wind. I curl my knees up to my chest and hug them. *Where the hell is everyone?*

I crane my neck to scan the island, but it's just brambles, moist sand, pieces of driftwood that have found their way here on the waves. One lone, bare tree with sprawling branches and a trunk the size of a small car sits behind me. It takes up most of the real estate on the island. Other than that, nothing. My backpack is gone. There's a draft on my back now and I tenderly bring my fingers there, running them over the neoprene. Great. There are slashes all down my wet suit, almost as if I've been mauled by a bear. I probe around with my finger and find blood. My hand is covered in blood. I turn around and there's a small puddle of it under my backside. Suddenly I'm aware of the sting.

Frantic, I search the river again. Nothing. No one. I'm

alone, in the middle of the rapids, bleeding. No. This is not good. My heart begins to pound so hard, I can almost hear it.

"Well, look who's wandering among the living."

I jump at the voice. Not that it's scary—it's just that two minutes ago, when I surveyed my surroundings, I was alone. Or at least I thought I was. The tree, though, has a large trunk, so maybe he was behind it. Yes, of course. Plus, my head hurts, so maybe I have a concussion and am not seeing things clearly. I turn, and a boy is loping toward me, easy, like he hasn't a care in the world. His light brown hair is falling in his face and he has this sheepish grin, like he's up to no good.

He sits down beside me and begins to pick at the line of white pebbles left by the tide. Those pearly little pebbles, the damp sand, our feet side by side at the water's edge— something about this scene gives me an instant shot of déjà vu that almost sends me reeling, like I'm falling through time and space. I catch myself, and by then he's studying me, that quirky smile melting into amused curiosity. "You talk?"

The voice. It's unsettling. Something is not quite right about it. It's an easy drawl, nothing like Justin's or Hugo's or that of any of the guys I know, and yet it sounds familiar. Anyone in this predicament, stuck in the middle of a river, would speak with a little bit of urgency. But then again, he's not the one who's bleeding.

My lips are so cold they tingle to life when I open them to speak. "I'm . . . hurt."

He nods and inspects the wound on my back. "Sure are."

He reaches out to touch it and I squirm a little when he comes in contact with the wound. "Ouch."

He doesn't apologize. "Tore up that little monkey suit of yours, too, huh?"

"It's a *wet* suit," I say miserably. "And a rental. I'll probably owe them an arm and a leg for it."

He's still inspecting it. There isn't a look of disgust on his face, or horror, so maybe it isn't that bad? I can feel his fingers stroking the fabric, which is really awkward, so I flinch away just as he says, "For that thing? Wouldn't trade you a piece of steamin' horse manure for it."

I stare at him. Who the hell talks like that? And weirder yet, why does it seem like I've heard this all before? "Wait. Do I know you?" I ask, but I already know that's impossible. He couldn't have been on the rafting excursion with us. All of the other people were older, and he's probably no more than twenty. He has a cologne-ad-pretty face with perfect features, just the right amount of stubble, and long eyelashes—a face that's hard to stop looking at, and even harder to forget. And he's not wearing a wet suit. In fact, he's not wearing much at all. Faded, ripped jeans and a worn plaid shirt, open, untucked, and with sleeves rolled up to the elbows. He's not wearing shoes. No shoes. It can't be more than forty degrees out today. Even Justin would have a hard time with that. "Aren't you freezing?"

He laughs. "No on both counts, kid."

At first I'm like, *Yeah, he's right, I'd remember a dude like him,* but the second he calls me "kid," the feeling hits me stronger than ever. I try to find the connection but my head is throbbing, making thinking impossible. And anyway, it doesn't matter. We're in the middle of a river, I'm gushing blood all over the place, and maybe the tide is changing and this little island won't be here an hour from now. "Look. I'm a little freaked out. I don't know where I am or where my friends are. You wouldn't happen to have a boat, would you?" I ask.

He grins at me, a slow grin. Why does he do everything slowly? And of course he doesn't have a boat. He doesn't even have *shoes*.

All right. *Think think think.* "How did you even get here, if you don't have a boat?" But I already know the answer. I echo him as he says, "I'm a powerful good swimmer."

He grins, and that's my cue to freak out. How did I know that?

"So, wait. I *do* know you?"

He shakes his head. "Listen, kid, you're wound up tighter than an eight-day clock. Relax for a minute."

"Relax!" I start, but then I stop. No, I don't know him, of course; I just hit my head or something and I'm not thinking straight.

He leans back, digging his palms in the dirt behind him. He's tall, like Justin; he stretches out with his legs crossed at the ankles in front of him, and his feet touch the water. Unlike me, he doesn't recoil from the cold of the river. I notice that his toes are a rather pleasing shade of brown. He has a tan. How can a guy in Maine in May have a tan? He doesn't look like the type to frequent tanning salons; he looks more like Justin in that regard. The manly-man type. But even the manliest of men can end up utterly screwed by nature. Rule number one: Nature always kicks ass.

"Um, look. I can't relax. You may be a *powerful good swimmer*, but I'm not. I'm hurt, and freezing, and I'm sure my friends are looking for me, so I need to get back to them. Can you help me?"

"Sure thing." Then he grimaces. I look down and for the first time I notice he's holding his arm, limp in front of him.

The blood is all over his hand. My blood? I lean forward. No, there's a massive gash on the top of his forearm, stretching almost from his elbow to his wrist bone. It's deep, too; the blood is a dark, thick purple. I gasp. "Oh my God."

He laughs at me. "It's nothing. Old war wound."

He's off his rocker. It's fresh. And it's bleeding everywhere. "No, you need . . ." I look around but there's no spare fabric anywhere, and I can't very well ask him to remove his worn shirt, since it's probably as thin as paper. Grimacing, I reach down and pull off my water shoes, then remove the outer layer of socks. They're damp, but they'll have to do. I wrap the first sock around his arm as a tourniquet. It's tough to tie because he happens to be kind of muscular there. Then I clamp the other one over the cut. It's instantly saturated. "We've got to get you help."

He looks at my handiwork. "Thanks, kid. But it's just fine."

It's really not just fine. We're both bleeding. We'll probably die here in a puddle of our own blood. "How did you do that, anyway?"

He shrugs. "Don't remember. Jumping in the water, I guess."

"To save me? You pulled me out?"

He stares at his arm. "That I did, but . . . I don't . . ." He looks confused, sad. "I don't remember lots of things."

"Well, thank you," I say. My sock is now dripping with blood. Little crimson drops begin to puddle on the sand. "Oh God. That's really bad. Are you sure you're okay?"

He laughs. "Unwind, girl. You want to see bad, you should have seen your back."

"What?" I shriek. Is it possible my wound is as bad? Um, worse? All this time I've been sitting here, I'd almost forgotten about it. It didn't even hurt much. I crane to see my injury, but I can't make out anything. In fact, I can't even feel it anymore.

He's still laughing.

I glare at him. "It's not that horrible, is it? You were joking? Don't. Do. That. You freaked me out. I thought I was dying."

"Unwind, girl. You need to—"

Suddenly thunder begins to rumble in the distance, and I realize that the clouds are black and heavy with rain. Across the river, a thin mist has crawled in, sliding between the trees. My eyes are drawn toward the right bank, where a figure stands, half hidden by the pines. I squint to see, but my head throbs as my eyes struggle to focus in the thickening fog. It's a large guy, like Justin, but I already know it's not him. Justin would be trying to find a way to help me. This person is standing still, and it would almost be like a fragment of a photograph if his eyes weren't trained right on us.

I feel a hand slide into mine, fingers lacing with my own. Next to me, the boy swallows. He's lost some of his tan. Since he obviously enjoys cold weather, I'd expected his hands to be warm, like Justin's. But they're cold, like stone. Unlike stone, though, his fingers quiver slightly. There's something wrong.

"Who is that?" I whisper.

He sits up, then pulls me to my feet so fast that I gasp in surprise. I'm stunned because it's the first thing he's done quickly. That easy smile is gone. I open my mouth to say "Well, now who's wound up?" but he speaks first, his words clipped and emotionless. "Nobody. Let's get you out of here. And, Kiandra—"

He grabs hold of my wrist and looks at me with intent, dark eyes. I want to ask him to let me go, I want to ask him how he knows my name, I want to ask him so many things, but the force of his eyes on me has rendered me speechless. Instead, I just nod, under this strange, dizzying spell.

"You have to go home. And don't you ever come back. It's too dangerous."

Whispers again. Just fragments of speech. This time I know they're senseless, so I don't bother to listen.

My eyelids sting as I push my eyes open. The sky again, gray and somber. Pine branches above, dulled in the fog. The mist is thicker now, borderline drizzle. My eyelashes are wet.

I feel for my limbs, wiggling my fingers and toes. My fingers ache from the cold, and my feet, in scratchy wool socks, ache, too. My face burns as if from a thousand needle pricks. I sit up, the same familiar pain slamming against my forehead, expecting to see the river on both sides of me. But I'm on the bank.

I turn around, but I'm alone. The boy who saved me is gone, but his voice is ringing in my ears: *Don't you ever come back. It's too dangerous.* What the . . . Who the heck was he? Hot as hell, but reminding me so eerily of my dad. Great combination.

I struggle to my numb feet and climb the bank, looking for him, for some sign of him, but there is nothing. It was a dream. It has to have been a dream. But all the while, I feel the pressure of his fingers on my back, and I can still hear his voice in my head—it makes me shiver.

No, it was just a dream. Normal people can have very realistic dreams, and that's all it was.

I climb a little farther, and just as I begin to wonder how I'm going to get back to camp, which must be miles downriver, I see a sign in the brush. I stumble over to it on my useless legs and read: NORTHEAST OUTFITTERS. There's an arrow pointing down a path, and the familiar rich wood of the cabin peeks from among the pines.

I want to cry from the beauty of it. I want to fall to my knees and thank the heavens. But I also want to be warm, and my legs must want that, too, because before I know what I'm doing, I've broken into a run. I racewalk, limping slightly because I can't feel much of my feet, toward the log building, throw open the doors, and burst into the Outfitters, gasping in relief as the heat rushes to my face. It stings my skin, but it's a welcome sting. The only thing better would be a nice, hot shower.

Angela and Hugo are sitting on the big leather sofa, nursing mugs of coffee. A fire roars in the fireplace, and I can already feel its heat. She jumps up when she sees me. "Oh my God, sweetie! Are you okay?"

I nod. "I'm just—"

She's not paying attention. She's already shoved Hugo off the couch and is propping up the pillows for me to lie down. She quickly kneels in front of me and commences with Operation Flo Nightingale. "Is there frostbite? Can you feel your toes?"

Before I can answer, she orders one of the men standing idle nearby to get her some blankets and a tub of warm water. Soon she's got pretty much everyone nearby helping out. She's truly in her element. Hugo's just standing there, and I half expect him to whip out his camera and start photographing my feet, which are a peculiar blue color, so I'm relieved when Angela orders him to go find Justin.

"Where is he?" I ask as Hugo runs outside.

"Looking for you, of course. He's out of his mind with worry. We have fifty people out there, all looking for you," Angela says. She stops rubbing my feet and studies me, then breaks into a sob. "Oh my gosh," she wails, covering her mouth with the back of her hand. "I was so worried about you! I really thought you were gone. You're not just my cousin, you're one of my best friends. If anything happened to you, I would never forgive myself."

"It's not your fault," I say, leaning over to pat her back.

"Uh-huh it is! We practically dragged you here." She wiggles my pinkie toe and I laugh, which I guess is a good sign, because she sighs with relief and moves on to the other foot. "We looked everywhere, but you just went under and you never surfaced. I've never seen anything like it. What happened to you?"

I shrug. I want to say something about that guy who saved me, but that must have been a hallucination. Everything about it seems tinged with gray, like an old dream. Like one of those visions I used to have long ago, when I lived in New Jersey. I think about that dark figure looming in the distance, across the river, and shudder. "I guess I blacked out. And when I woke up, I was on the riverbank, right by the Outfitters."

She wrinkles her nose. "That's, like, impossible."

"Why?"

"Because it's fifteen miles! You floated downriver in the cold for fifteen miles and your feet look like this? And somehow the river just deposited you right on the shore in front of the Outfitters?"

I stare at her. "What, you don't believe me?"

"No, I do. It's just a miracle," she says. "I've heard of people blacking out during times of extreme stress. Maybe you . . . I don't know. It's a miracle."

The door bursts open, sending a swirl of cold air into the cabin. Justin rushes in, with Hugo at his heels. "Is she okay?" Then he sees me. "Kiandra, are you okay?"

I'm about to speak, but Justin looks at Angela for confirmation. "Yeah," she says. "She seems okay."

"The paramedics will check you out," he says, his eyes wider than I've ever seen them. It looks like he's the one who needs medical help.

Suddenly I remember the blood oozing from my back. I'd been so comfortable on the sofa I'd forgotten about it. "Oh, I—I think I hurt my back." I lean forward and they both inspect it, moving me back and forth to see what I'm talking about.

Angela helps me pull off the wet suit. My limbs are kind of sore, but moving them feels good. The pain is a confirmation I'm alive. I sit there for a while in my long underwear, waiting for them to say something about how big the wound is or how it'll need stitches, but I wait, and wait. Finally, I look up at their faces. Angela is squinting, not in horror, but as if she's trying to see something on the point of a needle. Justin says, "Where?" and massages my shoulder. His hands are already warm, even though he'd just been out in the cold.

I hurt all over—but back there? No, it doesn't ache anymore. Could that have been a dream, too? "There's no blood?"

Someone comes with a couple of blankets. Angela throws one over me and says, "You should rest. You might have hit your head."

The wet suit is a puddle on the ground. I lean over and pick it up, turning it over in my hands. No holes. It was a dream. Just like the ones I had in Jersey. Those used to feel so real, I'd known some of the characters in them by name. I used to miss them when they weren't with me. I find myself flashing back to the girl in the white dress, walking along the river. Lannie.

I look up. They're all staring at me expectantly. "Um, what?"

Angela says, "I asked if you wanted something to eat." She looks between Justin and me. "You know what? I'll just get her a bagel. You guys talk," she says, and speeds off.

Justin kneels down on the braided rug beside me. "You scared me to death," he whispers, rubbing his face tiredly.

"I'm sorry," I say.

"It's not your fault. It's ours. I just— You're so light. I could carry three of you, if I wanted to. Why couldn't I pull you in?"

I shrug. "Maybe my foot was caught in the branches of a tree or something."

He nods, but the look on his face is doubtful. "And then how did you end up here?"

I explain to him what I told Angela. "She says it's a miracle that I made it after that long in the water."

He lets out a short laugh. "I'll say."

"So I should be dead?"

"I don't know. I've never had it happen before. The few times we lost people we were able to get them back in the boat within a couple of minutes. That water was, like, forty degrees. How did you . . . Oh, right. You blacked out." He exhales and runs his fingers through his hair. "Yeah. I thought you were probably dead."

He gives me the most pathetic look I've ever seen. For the first time, his eyes glisten a little, maybe from tears, but then I think I must be going crazy because Manly Justin does not cry.

"But I'm not," I say brightly, trying to take the edge off his misery.

"But you should be. You were gone for *three hours*, Ki. That's how long it takes to get down here from put-in. And you got dumped fifteen minutes into the ride. You don't float down the Dead River in May on nothing but your good looks and end up back home *alive*." He reaches under the wool blankets and wiggles one of my toes, like he's playing This Little Piggy. "And with all your cute parts still intact."

I shrug. "Just call me Miracle Girl."

He smiles. "Hell yeah, Miracle Girl. I'm so freaking relieved. How would I have explained this to your dad?"

Angela returns with a bagel with cream cheese and a mug of coffee. "You eat this and rest," she says. "I'm going to go back to our cabin and pack, and you guys come over after the paramedics have checked everything out."

I look at her. "Pack?"

Justin nods. "I think we'd better call it a weekend, don't you? You can't really want to . . ."

"No, it's okay," I say, wondering how I'd explain to my father why we came home from Baxter Park early. Besides, prom is tomorrow and it's too late to even think about going now. The words *Don't you ever come back. It's too dangerous* play somewhere in the back of my head, but that's no problem. It's not like I was planning to go rafting again. And besides, that was just a dream. "We were going to hike and stuff. I still want to do that. I don't want to ruin your weekend. You've planned it for so long."

"But—" Angela starts, and then looks at Justin.

"But really, I'm fine," I say. Plus, the idea of hanging out with Justin tonight, alone, sounds really good. I'm fine. And I'm not going to let a swim in the river and some stupid hallucination tell me where I can and can't go.

"All right," they say in unison, then look at each other and laugh.

I knew it wouldn't take much to convince them. After Ange leaves, I take a bite of my bagel, and then another, and before I know it, it's totally gone. I'm ravenous. I could eat another one. Maybe two. I also could probably sleep for fourteen hours, because my head feels heavy, almost like there's water in my ears. I try to stand up to get to the kitchen but Justin puts a firm hand on my shoulder. "I'll get you another, as long as you chew the next one before you swallow. The last thing I need is you almost dying *again*." He rolls his eyes like I'm a toddler in danger of ruining another perfectly good onesie.

I smile, thinking I have the best boyfriend in the world, then lean over to pick up my socks. I'm just stretching them out on the rug to let them dry when I realize something. I was wearing two pairs of heavy wool socks earlier. Now there is only one.

The other pair, I gave to that boy on the river. The boy who warned me to go away. The one I'd just convinced myself didn't exist.

CHAPTER NINE

Now I'm at the edge of the river, watching the waves with the girl in the white dress. She's crying. "Hi, Lannie," I say.

She smiles and wipes at her tears. "Tootsie. You came back. I can't believe you came back. And you remember me."

"Of course I do." I try to see where I am, but the sun is bouncing off the ripples in the water, drenching everything around me in white. "Where am I, though?"

She doesn't answer. Suddenly it's like I'm in a white room with no windows or doors. Just me, alone. But the name Jack rings in my ears. I've never known anyone with that name, at least not until . . . No, it's familiar. I did hear it, once before, quite recently. Jack McCabe.

Sleesh . . . sleesh . . . sleesh.

Only a second later the story comes to me. I see the girl, dressed all in white, strolling into the woods. Lannie. And he's watching, close behind, his eyes dark and intense.

The man from across the river. Jack. Jack McCabe.

I did everything you asked of me.

Somehow, it's dark now. He follows Lannie, deeper into the forest, toward the river, toward her. I follow, too, stumbling over the brambles and uneven ground. Lannie stops by the river, standing still at the very edge. I watch as Jack approaches, expecting him to call out to her, to reach for her. Instead, at the moment he's supposed to do that, he turns. Lannie turns. They're both looking at me.

Blood is trickling over Jack's forehead, making an upside-down Y over the sides of his nose. Lannie has the ax. It's covered in blood. "Everything's wrong," she seethes. "Because of you."

At first I don't know who she's speaking to, but her eyes are on me. "Wait—" I say.

But she is storming toward me, ax raised over her head. Hatred disfigures her pretty face. Hatred for me?

Jack doesn't move. "I did everything you asked of me," he whispers, a tinge of sadness in his voice, but by then she is upon me.

I wake with a start, expecting to hear the blade whistle down on me. Instead, the fire crackles. Far away, people are laughing. It's warm, and the orange light of the fire is homey and inviting. A cuckoo clock cuckoos. I look down. My second bagel, slathered in cream cheese, is sitting on the coffee table. Justin is leaning forward, staring at me. "Nice nap?" he asks.

Yeah. Real nice.

I wipe my eyes and reach for my mug of coffee. It's cold and bitter but I sip it anyway.

"The paramedics are here," he says.

I sit up and two men poke me, take my vitals, and, as I

91

expected, tell me I'm perfectly healthy. I wonder if that's what they'd see if there was a test they could do on my mind. Because the dreams, the dreams I used to have when I was a kid, when I lived by the water . . . I might be completely wrong, but that felt a lot like one of them. One of the bad ones.

"You okay?" Justin asks after we pack up our stuff and start walking back toward Angela's place. By then, the sun must have come out, because it's sinking beyond the tall pines on the other side of the river, painting the whole sky the color of flames.

I nod. "I just want to get back to the cabin. Take a hot shower."

He winces. "Ooh, sorry. You know Angela's place doesn't have running water."

"Oh." I want a shower so bad, I can almost taste the hot steam, feel it curling around my body as the water rinses the grimy river away. My skin is gritty, dirty. I take my hair out of the ponytail holder and try to comb it back with my fingers, but they stick in the mess of knots and dirt and who-knows-what in there. I might have a colony of something living in my hair follicles. I hang my shoulders and a tear slips out of the corner of my eye.

"You can take a shower back at the Outfitters," he says brightly. "Hey, how about this. I'll go get your bag, and you go back there and tell Spiffy. He'll set you up." He winks. "It'll be the—"

I glare at him. "Highlight of his young life, I know. Shut up."

"I'm just kidding. But seriously. I'll walk you over. They have nice showers there. And Spiffy won't peek." He smiles. "That much."

I punch him, but I go along with it anyway. "I can make it myself. You go on," I say, giving him a kiss. His hand lingers on mine for a while before he lets it go, and after taking only one step toward the cabin, he turns right back, just to make sure I really am okay. He exhales slowly, and I know he's thinking he almost lost me.

When I leave him, I can't help picking up the pace. Showers! A chance to brush my teeth! To look and feel normal again! Just the thought of it sends me skipping back along the path.

I find myself slowing, even before my mind catches up with what is happening. I look up and across the river. Among the trees, their new leaves whipping in the wind, I see him.

The man across the river. Jack. He's standing still, as in my dream.

Watching me.

No, I think, my body turning to ice. *It's him. He's real.*

I turn down the path, wishing Justin, or *anyone,* were nearby and could see him, too. But once again I am alone. I start to walk again, knees weak this time, when out of nowhere a hand falls on my shoulder.

I gasp as a nearby voice says, "You should leave. I told you to, kid."

The boy I'd spoken to on the island. He's bleeding from that wound I thought I'd wrapped. It's not wrapped now. The blood is dripping on his bare foot.

"I'm not going anywhere. You are not real," I whisper.

But he's so close. So, so close. He leans in, even nearer. If he's not real, why do I feel his breath on my cheek?

He extends a long finger, pointing directly to where Jack is standing. "He's got his hooks in you already? Geesh. I thought you were stronger than that, kid. You *are*. You just don't get it. Suppose I'm gonna have to learn you what's what. Never thought I'd have to learn a Levesque girl."

I stare at his oozing wound. A wound he barely seems to notice. "You're . . . still bleeding."

He narrows his eyes. "Are you listening to anything I say?"

"What is your name?" I ask.

"Now's not the time for proper introductions."

"You know my name, somehow. I want to know yours," I say bitterly.

"It's Trey," he says quickly, but somehow I already knew that. Trey. The boy from the story. These people are all from the stories I heard over the campfire last night. *Ghost* stories. Ever since I heard them, I've been hallucinating. But why? Before I can ask another question, he speaks. "You love your boyfriend?" he asks.

"What?" I say. As if it's any of his business. But the thing is, I don't even wonder how he knows so much about me. It's almost like I expected him to know everything. Because he is just a part of my imagination, right? "Why am I talking to you? You're not r—"

"Do you?" He positions himself squarely in front of me so that his eyes bore into mine. His blood drips on my hiking boots, seeping between the laces. For someone who isn't real, his words hit me hard.

I bite my tongue. "Yes."

"You love your life? You love your daddy? You want to get back home to him?"

I nod. "Yeah. Of course. What—"

"Then you need to hightail it out of here while you still can, girl. Don't make me—"

I'm snapped back into reality when a bird caws in the trees. I turn and Spiffy is staring at me. The boy I was just talking to is gone. *Whoosh.* Vanished.

"Hi there," Spiffy says gently. "Sorry you had such a crap time out there. Not one of our better days on the Dead."

For a second, everything is out of focus, and when I finally come back, I have to grab Spiffy's shoulder to stop myself from falling over. He steadies me. "Still woozy, I guess," I lie.

"You should probably lie down," he says, his voice slightly condescending.

I swallow, wondering how much he witnessed. Did he see me talking to that guy? Judging from the way his eyebrows are raised, it's very likely he saw me talking, all right—to nobody. I want to grab him and ask him if he sees Jack across the river, but by then Jack is gone. I'm back in the land of the living. "I thought maybe I could grab a shower?" I ask, my voice cracking because I'm trying too hard to not sound insane.

He brightens. "Hey. Yeah. Sure. This way."

I follow him, but now even the idea of a shower doesn't sound so great. Because now, I really don't want to be alone. Alone . . . with *them.*

CHAPTER TEN

I wipe away the steam on the mirror but don't recognize the face there. I scrubbed and scrubbed the river grime from my body in the shower, but no amount of scrubbing could wash away the voices in my head. The visions didn't attack me while I was washing, but I couldn't help worrying that they would. If Jack and Trey and the others would rip back the shower curtain and say, "Surprise!"

The thought makes me quiver. My eyes are sunken, and maybe it's the fluorescent light or the deep creases in my forehead, but I don't look very pretty anymore. And I can't help wondering what it was my mother heard, what my mother saw, that made her walk into the river that day. Maybe she didn't go willingly. Maybe she . . .

No, that's stupid. She killed herself. End of story.

As I spread my toiletries along the glass shelf, I wonder if things would have been different if I had insisted on going to the prom. Hell, of course they would have. If I'd had a backbone. If I'd told Justin what I wanted.

I think of what that boy said to me. *I thought you were stronger than that.* Then I shake it away. I don't want to think about him, about what one of my stupid visions said. They're from *stories*. They're not real. What do they know?

I don't have a hair dryer, so I towel-dry my hair and tie it up in a loop at the top of my head, then brush my teeth and throw on a bulky sweatshirt and jeans and my North Face jacket. I was hoping the shower would make me feel more comfortable, but I still feel . . . icky. Wrong.

When I step into the main room, Justin is waiting for me. "Feel good?"

He grabs me into a bear hug and gives me a peck on the nose. I smell peppermint and shaving cream. He must have showered, too. "Yeah. Better."

Though not much.

We walk outside and immediately I smell chicken roasting. Smoke billows from a spot over the hill, near the river, and a bunch of people are congregating at picnic benches. We start to walk there, but I stop. I don't want to be anywhere near the river. I don't want to be where I can hear the whispering. Where I can look across the river and see *him*.

Justin senses something and hangs back. "Not hungry?"

I look down at my hands. They're shaking. I'm pathetic.

Real or not, that guy was right. I am stronger than that. At least, I should be. And maybe if I can prove they don't frighten me, the visions will leave me alone.

I take a step forward. "No, I am," I say, picking up the pace.

I can ignore the whispers. And if he's there, I'll just ignore him. Besides, it's not like they're real. They can't do anything to me. They've never done anything to me before.

By the time we make it to the picnic benches, my mouth is watering. We grab a couple of Cokes and stand in line. There's a Tupperware container of dill spears. As I'm sucking a pickle into my mouth, a camera clicks. Oh no. Hugo. I can just see the next issue of the school newspaper, with my face on the front page.

"Would you stop—" I whirl around, fully prepared to stab him with my plastic fork, when I'm faced with an older man I've never seen before. He has a way-more-professional-looking camera and a way-less-smarmy-looking expression than Hugo's. I step back. "Oh."

"You're the one, right?" he says, his words coming out kind of garbled because he's trying to uncap a pen with his mouth while juggling his equipment.

I just stare at him.

He finally manages to get his things under control and extends a hand. "Mark Evans, *Portland Press Herald*. Heard about your little swim."

Oh. My. God. "No, I—" But I don't know what to say. All I know is that my dad always starts off his morning with two things: a bowl of Cheerios and a copy of the *Portland Press Herald*. And the last thing he needs is to find his daughter's picture on the front page when he's expecting her to be hiking at Baxter State Park.

This is not good.

"You've got the wrong girl," Justin says behind me. "I think I saw her over near the front office."

"Oh. Thanks," the man says, hurrying off.

I turn to Justin, surprised. He's usually the last person to catch on to anything; thinking on his feet, lying—these things come about as easily to him as rocket science. He grins at me. "My girlfriend, the celebrity. What do you say we get our food to go? The Bruins are on tonight. Playoff hockey."

"That sounds just fantastic," I joke. He knows how little I like to watch hockey, how much Wayview's obsession with the sport drives me crazy.

We get two plates heaping with chicken, corn, and coleslaw, and head back up to the cabin. "That was a close one, huh? Don't know what I would have told your dad."

I shrug. "My dad likes you."

"That will change easily if he finds out about this."

"He won't find out. And we went over this. Rafting is as safe as bowling. His fears of this place are completely irr—" I stop. I can't really say they're irrational anymore. Not after what happened today.

"It sucks that we had to lie to get you up here. I mean, it'd make a cool story. When I was waiting for you to take a shower, I heard all the guides talking about you. Some of them have been on the river for a dozen years and have never seen anything like it. They're pretty sure you have ice water running through your veins."

"Really?" I kind of like that. It makes me sound tough.

"Yep. They all want you even more now."

"Oh, shut up!" I say, nearly dropping my Coke as I'm elbowing him in the ribs.

"All right. But still, it would have been sweet to see your cute mug on the front page. And a headline. 'The Ice Girl Cometh' or something."

I think about it. I guess that would be cool. But the reporter would ask question after question, wanting to know how I survived the ordeal, and I wouldn't be able to answer any of them. Nobody knows what happened on the river, least of all me. And part of me doesn't want to know. "If my father knew, he'd kill me," I whisper.

"I know, I know. Why do you think he's so afraid of rafting, but he'd let you hike the Knife Edge in Baxter?" he muses as we climb the steps toward the cabin and stand at the edge of the highway, waiting for a pickup to pass. "The Knife Edge is not exactly kiddie play. People die there, you know."

I shrug. I can't explain that my dad would prefer me dangling from high-rises to even *smooth* sailing. Justin and I have been going out long enough, and I suppose I could tell him. Tell him that my mom walked into the Delaware one summer and never returned. But I'm not speaking of her. I refuse to let her have any bearing on my life right now, despite what my dad wants.

We step into the cabin and out of the chilly early May air. I set my plate of food on the small table in the foyer, let down my hair and start shaking it out, only to bump into Justin. He's standing like a massive tree trunk in the center of the hall. I try to shove him but I realize he's dropped his plate of food. On his feet. And yet he doesn't seem to have noticed that. He's just standing there, frozen.

"Justin, you—" I start, but then I realize what has captured his interest.

"Hi, guys!" Angela springs up from the probably-fake bear rug at the center of the great room. She's trying to straighten her rumpled T-shirt and wipe her mouth at the same time. Hugo gets up behind her. Both of them are all red, like they've been . . .

Yikes.

"Damn!" Justin shouts, like, twenty seconds too late, jumping back and looking at the mess on the floor. We both stoop down and start picking barbecue chicken and coleslaw off his hiking boots. "I mean, um, sorry if we were . . ."

"Oops," I say, grinning at Angela. I take Justin's plate and throw it in the trash, then pick up mine, trying my best to be quick about it. "You know, don't mind us. We'll just, um, take all this stuff and go upstairs. Okay?"

Angela looks totally embarrassed. She starts to argue, but then Hugo, who growls as if he's about to kill us for disturbing them, pulls on her wrist. "Um, all right," she says.

Justin plucks a corn kernel out of his laces. "Yeah. You guys . . . As you were, soldiers," he mutters in an authoritative voice, taking my hand and pulling me up the stairs.

"What about your food?" I ask.

"What about it?"

"Do you want to get more?" I ask, but by then he's slammed

the door behind me and has pushed me up against the bureau. I struggle to put my plate down as his hands find their way under my jacket. They're warm but his skin is rough against my belly and so it tickles. When he pushes his tongue into my mouth, I can't stop laughing.

He pulls away. "What?"

Oh, how can I explain it without hurting him? When Justin kisses me, his tongue probes my mouth, so I rarely get a chance to kiss back. And his hands are so big and pawlike, they don't touch me in a way that elicits shivers. The words "Justin" and "romantic" are opposites. I don't know if the stuff from romance novels is real, if it can be real to have a guy who is caring *and* who makes me feel weak in the knees. Justin is smart, sweet, and stable, which are all good things. He'll never be the one to make me swoon, but some things are more important than romance.

I ask between kisses, "Um, why this sudden interest in making out?"

He nibbles on my ear. "The adrenaline. It's killer."

"But I'm hungry," I say, pushing him away gently. "And sleepy."

He pulls away, his eyes searching mine for a moment. Then he says, "Right. Sorry. You've had a crazy day. You should get your sleep."

I wrap my arms around him and give him a big kiss on the lips. "Will you stay with me?"

As an answer, he pulls me closer. That night, we share my plate of chicken, though he lets me have most of it. I try to come up with a poem about my trip down the river but end up writing only three words in my notebook, words said to me by a figment of my imagination: *It's too dangerous.* Then I fall asleep in Justin's arms, with the sound of the hockey game in the background. With his arms around me, I'm almost unafraid to close my eyes. But I know there's little he can do to protect me from the things he cannot see. And he can't protect me from myself.

CHAPTER ELEVEN

The early sunlight glows orange through the trees. When I wake, the house is so silent I can hear the ticking of the clock in the kitchen echoing through the open-floor-plan space. It's still quite dark outside; the trees are a single black-green mass against the orange background. I sit up and pry Justin's heavy arm off my body, but he doesn't stir, just pushes the side of his face deeper into the pillow.

Downstairs, Hugo and Angela are still sleeping, their bodies wrapped together in such a way that I'm almost ashamed to look, even though they're fully clothed. I shudder. Angela, Angela, Angela. I may be going crazy, but I'd never be so insane as to think that Hugo was someone I'd want to be that close to.

I check through the kitchen cabinets and find some whole coffee beans, but I have no clue how to grind them. Then I remember that the Outfitters had some coffee. I'm sure they wouldn't mind me bumming a cup. After all, I'm the miracle girl. I'll just have to avoid any reporters.

Reporters and . . . unsavory and possibly imaginary characters, I think as I step out into the chilly morning. It's actually warmer than yesterday, and now the sun is starting to peek through the trees more. I jog down the driveway and across the highway, avoiding the river. The sound of my running shoes on the gravel effectively drowns out the gentle hum of the current. I don't stop until I'm in the Outfitters. But as I'm pulling open the door, I catch sight of that photo in the glass case, and I hear it.

What the devil is that?

"Don't you start, Uncle Robert," I mutter as I step inside.

It's just as busy as yesterday. A new group of adventurers is suiting up for the river. Some faces look familiar, but most are strange. They don't know that I'm *the one*. That's a good thing. A guy who is standing at the door looks at me growling to nobody and assumes I'm talking to him. He scoots aside, apologizing so effusively for being in my way that I feel bad. I blush and try to explain that I wasn't talking to him, but stop. Maybe it's for the best that he think I was talking to him. Better to be a bitch than a nutcase.

"Hey! Ice Girl!" a voice calls. It's Spiffy. He's wearing what I think is the same outfit he had on yesterday, and looking like he slept in a tree. "How are you? Ready for Round Two?"

I blush more, embarrassed. So they really are calling me that. "Um, not in a million years, thanks. I came for the coffee."

He laughs and points to the kitchenette. "Just made a fresh pot."

I inhale the heavenly scent of the beans as I start to cross the room, but freeze when I see who is there, pouring himself a cup. He has his back to me but the thick strap of his camera is wrapped around his neck, so I know it's him. I curse and turn around quickly. Spiffy notices, so I say, "I don't want that guy to see me. He wants to do a story on me for the *Herald*."

Spiffy watches him. "Don't worry. You're old news. He has a better scoop."

"Really?" I exhale and loosen, wondering how that could've happened so quickly. I know news moves fast, but this is kind of ridiculous. "Which is?"

"When they were combing the river looking for you, they found another body."

I put my hands over my mouth. They must have found Uncle Robert. "Oh my God. I'm so sorry."

He shrugs, a bewildered look on his face. "They just found some bones. That's all they know right now."

"Oh! I thought . . . I mean, I thought it was your uncle."

He stares at me. "No. He's hiking the Trail." Then he eyes me with mock suspicion. "Unless you know something we all don't."

"No, I just . . . um, nothing," I say, hurrying to the kitchenette. By the time I get there, my cheeks and the back of my neck are burning. I pour the coffee and immediately try to take a sip, but it scalds my tongue. I stand there, inhaling the aroma, trying to wake up so I can spare myself any more awkward exchanges like that. Spiffy must think I'm insane enough already. And he'll think it all the more when they discover that those bones are his uncle Robert. This I know, just as well as I know my own name. But they don't need to hear it from me. I'm already Ice Girl. I don't need to be Oracle Girl, too.

It's getting pretty crowded and the room is buzzing with adrenaline-pumped adventure seekers, so I quickly make my exit, wrapping my hands around the Styrofoam cup to keep them warm. Immediately the waves start to whisper.

"Why can I hear you, Uncle Robert?" I mutter in the general direction of the river.

"The river only talks to people worth talking to."

As I whirl around, hot coffee froths from the top of the cup, spraying my hands. I wince at the pain, steady the cup, and bite my sore tongue.

Because standing in front of me is Jack McCabe.

CHAPTER TWELVE

I squeeze my eyes shut. I push hard against my eyeballs with my thumb and forefinger. I chant, "You're not real. You're not real. You're not real."

I'm going to continue on. I'm going to push past him and get back to my boyfriend, then never leave Justin's side again. I try to move, but it's not fast enough.

All the while, Jack is very near. He doesn't float; his footsteps are soft, but they're there. I can feel his breath on my neck. I can feel his smooth fingertips prying my hand from my face, lacing his fingers with my own. Something touches my cheek; it is cold as ice, yet it sends a white-hot shock down to my toes. The icy-hot sensation trails toward my mouth. His lips. He presses them against mine, not really delivering the kiss, just . . . lingering, until I have this overwhelming urge to finish it, to pull him hard to me, to beg him to feed his tongue into me. But suddenly the force is gone, and the cold breeze that slips between us, warm compared to his lips, is like a slap on my face.

I open my eyes. He is still there. It's just me and him, on the path. From here I can see the Outfitters, and the cabin, and yet I am helplessly alone with him. Whatever he is.

"Do you believe I'm real now?" he says, a small smile tugging at his lips.

I nod, shivering. "Are you a ghost?"

"You're not like the others. You're much more in tune with the river than they are. They don't see or hear the things you do."

"But why?"

"Ah, Mistress. You mean no one has explained it to you?"

Mistress? Is that a term of endearment? "No," I mutter.

"All right. Then I will."

I take a deep breath, which calms me a little. Just a little. Not so much that my entire body isn't shaking, but enough so that my voice comes out even. "So, explain."

He holds up a finger, scolding me as if I were a child. "You need patience."

"Maybe you need to be a little less mysterious," I counter.

He raises his eyebrows. "All right. I'll give you that. What are your questions?"

"The river," I say. "It always sounds like it's whispering."

"They have something to say to you."

"They? Who are *they*?"

"Let them tell you. They want to tell you. Just listen."

"I've tried," I say. "Most of the time it's just pieces, fragments. It doesn't make any sense."

"They're all trying to speak to you at once. The longer and

closer you listen, the more you'll be able to make out the individual voices."

"But who are they?"

He doesn't say anything, but I already know. I don't know if I could stand to hear the answer. And there's something strange about the way he's staring at me so intently, as if he's waited all his life to have this conversation with me. Which is crazy, because I've only just met him. "Who are you?"

"I heard your friends telling the story. The story of my life and, it seems, my untimely death." He laughs. "Don't look so shocked. I said I was real. But I never said I was still alive."

My heart shudders in my chest. "So you are a . . . ghost?"

"Well, I wouldn't use that term. I prefer to say that I'm traveling on a different plane. But I suppose 'ghost' is what humans would call me, yes."

"Then why can I see you?"

"Correct me if I'm wrong, but you can see and hear all of us, can you not? That's why all the voices are in your head, and you're having a hard time sorting them out."

"All of who?"

"All of those who met their fate on the water," he answers. "Because we need you. *She* needs you."

My breath hitches. "She?"

"The whispers you've heard," he says. "Surely one of the voices you've heard has sounded familiar?"

I shake my head. That the river is whispering at all is so much to wrap my brain around, I haven't had time to think that a voice might be familiar to me. "I don't . . . I don't think so." I murmur, but all at once I know what he is going to say. And as sure as I'm standing there, I know it's the truth.

"It's your mother," he says. "And she has been waiting for you."

"My mother?" I repeat, the word sounding strange coming off my tongue since I haven't uttered it in nearly a decade. "But she died in New Jersey."

"All waterways are connected. And her body was never found, yes? So she is one of us. She is here."

"Here? You're crazy." My voice quavers. So much for the idea of keeping the Nia Levesque legend five hundred miles away. I can only think back to her funeral. The coffin was empty. In it, we placed her favorite necklace and a scarf she always wore, and a picture of all of us together. My father never said as much, and we never discussed it, but obviously the body hadn't been found. She wasn't the first person lost on the river whose body was never recovered. "Then where is she?"

"I've come to take you to her," he says, extending his hand to me.

Instinctively I reach out to grab it, but a breeze picks up, skittering old leaves down the path and digging under my hairline, sending a chill down my back. When I touch them, his fingers are so icy they sting. I try to pull my hand away, but he clamps his fingers tight on mine, squeezing like a vise. Then he begins to pull me toward the river. The river that I hate, that nearly killed me. I try to dig my heels into the gravel, but he's too strong. I try to steady the hot coffee I'm still holding, but it's splashing up over the sides of the cup, scalding my hand. I look down the path, but even though the place is normally so busy early in the morning, there is no one around. "Hey! What are you—"

"You want to see her, don't you?" He continues to pull me.

Panic rises in my voice as I squeak out, "Where are we going?" But I know the answer. Not twenty yards separates us from the river, and there is nothing else in between but a rocky embankment.

He means to take me *into the river*. He means to drown me. The cup flies out of my grasp, splattering hot liquid over his forearm, but he doesn't flinch, even as steam rises from the black droplets on his skin. I'm fighting now, trying to pry his fingers off mine with my other hand, but it's useless. Soon I'm begging, pleading with him to stop, but he doesn't listen. Finally, I gather all the strength I can into my arms and yank myself away. I'm free, but when I take a step back my foot lands awkwardly on a fallen branch, twisting. Pain tears through my ankle. I yelp and fall to the ground.

I massage the ankle, but the pain intensifies with my touch. He bends over me and slides my sock down over my heel. I don't want him to touch my ankle. I don't want to feel those icy fingers of his, stroking my skin. It will only confuse me. Because he feels so real. But he can't be. This is all in my mind. When I pull my sock up and scoot away from him, the pain shoots up to my knee. "Don't touch it."

His face is rueful; it almost makes me regret not letting him help me. "You want to see your mother, don't you?" he asks, his voice gentle. "She's just across the river."

I think of Spiffy's words. I know what lies on the other side of the river. He said people lived on the east side, but they buried their dead on the other side. "I don't . . . no. She's dead. The dead are there. I'm not dead. And you're not real."

"I thought we went over this." He studies me, a look of disappointment on his face. "I assure you, I am very real. And she is waiting for you, just over there. There is nothing for you to be afraid of."

As he reaches for my hand again, another wind picks up. "I can't—I can't cross the river."

A look of amusement dawns on his face. "*You* are afraid of the water?"

"No," I answer curtly. "But I can't cross the river without a boat."

He scans the shoreline, scratching his chin. "Ah. The unique problems of the living." He gives me a warm smile. "Forgive me, Kiandra. It has been quite some time since I've been on your plane."

As he laughs, a thick trickle of blood starts to ooze over his forehead. I watch it trail over the tip of his nose, but he seems oblivious to it until I point it out with my quivering hand.

He takes a handkerchief out of his pocket and dabs at it. "Oh, how embarrassing."

"It was your father who did that?" I ask softly. "I remember it from the story."

He studies the new blood on the handkerchief, but now more is pouring past his hairline, falling between his eyes. "No. That story your companions told is a little, shall we say, inaccurate. I suppose it served its purpose. But sometimes a lie is better."

"I don't understand how all these stories we told around the campfire the other night are haunting me," I say. "They're *stories.*"

"They were legends. They *did* happen, long ago. And legends get twisted over time. And you don't just know our stories. You know *all* the stories of the people who've died in the waters. That is part of your gift. You just need something to awaken the memory, I suppose. But it's all inside you, waiting to be released." He taps on the side of my head, sending droplets of blood scattering onto his shirt. I gasp and step back.

Suddenly he stops, looks around. I hear it, too: *Sleesh . . . sleesh . . . sleesh.*

He sighs. "I must go. I have something to attend to. I will see you again."

I nod, but it's not like I ever want to see him again. Seeing him again means I'm crazy.

He starts to walk down the path toward the river, and it's only then that I realize he's carrying the ax. The blade is brown with dried blood. "Oh, and Kiandra. Next time, I will prove your mother is waiting for you. And you will come."

You will come. I shiver when I think of it. He seems so confident. Much more confident than I am.

But the thing is, I was perfectly happy knowing my mother is gone forever.

And I don't want a next time.

CHAPTER THIRTEEN

Across the river, something gleams yellow, like gold.

It makes me think of my mother, of my bedroom, of the setting sun sparkling gold on the river outside. She grew up on the river. She'd moved away for a time, before college, but she'd found her way back. "I love the river," she told me. "I love it to my bones. I never want to be anywhere but here."

My father didn't like the river. We moved there when I was five, and in the two years we lived there, the basement of our old house flooded about a hundred times. It was so permanently moldy and dank that we never went down there. The foundation of our house was crumbling because of the water damage. He kept telling her we should "sell the damn thing before it collapses on us." My mother and father rarely argued, since my mom, being prone to headaches, tried hard to keep the peace. But when they did fight, it was about the house. "A river symbolizes purity," she'd tell me. "To a river, every day is a new day, a chance to start over. Isn't that a comforting thought?"

"Mom," I'd ask. "Why do you want to start over?"

She'd laugh. "I don't want to. But sometimes things end. And it's comforting to be able to begin again."

At the time, that made no sense to me. *Sometimes things end.* Afterward, I always thought about it bitterly. I mean, did she think that she could somehow just undo drowning herself in the river? But now Jack, a ghost or a vision or whatever he is, is telling me she's here. That she is waiting for me. And though I know it's simply crazy, it's all I can think about.

Sometime later, and I really don't know how much later, I hear Justin shuffling down the path. I'm sitting at a picnic bench, nursing a nearly empty container of coffee and staring across the river.

My mother can't be there. And I can't see her again. She's dead, and people aren't supposed to see the dead.

But I saw Jack. It wasn't like he was a vapor, a ghost. He was beside me. *Traveling on another plane,* and yet real. I could feel his breath, his cold, cold skin.

Is my mother that real? Could I possibly—

"Hey, you." Justin's voice startles me. "I see you were up bright and early."

I stare at him for a good long time, still lost in thought. The smile on his face is just beginning to break down into concern when I blink twice and come alive. "Oh. Um, yeah."

"Angela made pancakes, if you want some." He points to the cup on the picnic table. "Does that taste like yesterday's sewage? I made a pot back at the ranch that's pretty good."

"Oh, okay. Thanks." I spill what's left of my coffee on the

ground, throw the cup in a nearby trash can, then follow him toward the cabin.

"What do you say to a hike today?" he asks. "You feeling up to it?"

I stretch my back. For the first time I realize it's not just my ankle that aches. I'm sore from head to toe. I feel every bit as if I've been tossed down a raging river with a bunch of logs and debris using me as a Ping-Pong ball. I totally don't want to be a wet blanket, though. I'm the one who insisted we stay, because I wanted to spend time with Justin. And here, all I've been doing is spending time alone, with my imaginary "friends." "Yeah. Of course."

I'm dragging behind him, so he turns and watches me walk a few steps. "Why are you limping?"

"I'm just a little sore," I say. "No big deal."

He points down at my foot. "You weren't limping yesterday. The paramedics—"

At first I'm not really sure how it happened. Then I remember trying to escape Jack, and him nearly putting his hand on my ankle. I shiver. "Um, I twisted my ankle a little this morning," I say. "But I'll just put an ice pack on it for a few minutes. It'll be okay."

"Well, Pleasant Pond Mountain isn't too tough of a hike. It's only eight miles." He reaches down and touches it. "That hurt?"

"Ouch!"

"I'll take that as a yes," he says. "You are staying home. I'll stay with you."

"Give me a break. Go hiking."

"I can't leave you here alone. What if you need something?"

"I'm not a quadriplegic." I give him a teasing look. "Look me in the eye and tell me you'd rather spend today nursing your clumsy oaf of a girlfriend."

He laughs. "Well, okay. But the good news is, you have a big-screen TV to keep you company, and I hear that tonight the Outfitters will be playing *The River Wild* out on the terrace. That's fun, right?"

"Totally," I say, forcing myself to smile.

Angela is standing in the cabin's foyer, in jeans and hiking boots, stuffing granola bars into her backpack. "I was just coming— Oh!" she gasps when she sees me. "Honey Bunches, you okay?"

I collapse into the nearest chair. "It's just a little sprain. It should be fine tomorrow."

"But, honey, we should go home, then, right?" She looks at Justin, then back at me. "I mean, this can't be any fun for you, can it?"

"No," I say. "All you've done for months is talk about this trip. And I am having a good time. Really. When you guys get back, we'll all watch the movie together. It'll be fun." They're both staring at me like I have bugs crawling out of my nose, so I say, "Where's Hugo?"

Angela motions to the bathroom. "Remember that liter of Absolut Justin brought?"

"Yeah?"

"Well, now it's a quarter of a liter. He's been puking all

morning. And there's no water in that bathroom. He'll be cleaning it up, not me." She groans, then raises her voice: "Did you hear me, Hugo? You. Are. Cleaning. It. Up!"

"Oh." For the first time, I hear noises coming from the downstairs bathroom. I'm kind of glad he took the Absolut off our hands, because I'm not in the mood to celebrate, and anyway, I do not need the help of anything that might further loosen my grasp on reality. "So I guess it's just you two?"

Justin nods. "You sure you're going to be—"

"Just go," I command, waving them away. "Have fun."

He gives me a peck on the top of the head, and they gather up their backpacks and head out. I smile after them until the guilt dims the brightness in my face. I sit there for a moment, massaging my ankle. It honestly doesn't feel as bad as I might have made it out to be. And that's a good thing. Because I have a feeling that for what I'm planning, I'm going to need it.

CHAPTER FOURTEEN

Ten minutes later, Hugo saunters out of the downstairs bathroom, scratching his backside. He looks pretty okay for someone who just spent hours worshipping at the porcelain shrine. He has a rolled-up *Sports Illustrated* and is whistling.

I expect to smell something disgusting coming from the open door, but I can't make anything out. "Did you clean in there?" I ask.

He jumps sky high, like a cartoon character that has stuck its finger in an electric socket. "What the hell are you doing here?"

I don't answer. "You can open a window, at least. And there's some 409 under the kitchen sink." I march over to the bathroom to inspect it, knowing it'll be gross. I can already tell from the way Hugo threw his McDonald's hamburger wrappers all over Monster that he isn't the cleanest person on earth. Holding my breath, I stand in the doorway and take the quickest of peeks. Then I open my eyes wide.

It's spotless.

I turn to him. He's still fanning himself with the rolled-up magazine from the shock of seeing me. "What?" he says.

"You weren't sick?"

"Yeah, I was. Of course I was. Why would I lie about that?"

"I don't know. All I know is, this bathroom is sparkly clean, and you don't strike me as the domestic type. Plus, you didn't have any cleaning supplies, dirty paper towels—"

"Okay, Sherlock, you got me," he sneers. "I just didn't want to go on a crummy hike today. What about you? Why are you here?"

"I twisted my ankle," I say, reaching down to massage it, though it really doesn't hurt anymore.

"You didn't want to go, either," he says, collapsing on a leather couch. "Face it. You see it, too."

I stare at him. Is it possible that Hugo, stupid, idiotic Hugo, could see some of the things I see? "See what?"

"Angela and Justin. Justin and Angela." When my face is just as blank as before, he says, *"In lurve."*

"What?" I start to laugh. Of course this wasn't about the ghosts. But still, I know what he's talking about. My laughter quickly dissolves. "What would make you think that?"

"You never noticed? They're always giving each other looks."

"Yeah, but they're best friends. She's not his type. Believe me," I say, as much to convince myself as to convince him. "I mean, I can see where you would think that, because I've thought it, too. But really. It's nothing."

He shrugs.

"Really. They've known each other since they were three," I say, thinking back to the time three years ago when we'd been making out in the yearbook office for the first time and Justin said, "Angela has nothing to do with this." How many times have I repeated that to myself over the years? She's his best friend, and that's it.

Angela is my closest friend. She was happy when she found out Justin and I were a couple. Happy. She bounced around and giggled like she was on bath salts. "I always thought you'd make a great couple," she said.

"Angela has nothing to do with this," I find myself saying.

"Huh?" Hugo's staring at me.

I grab my backpack and step over his legs, which are sprawled out on the coffee table. "I've got something to do."

"Your poor, throbbing ankle all better?" he asks with a crafty grin. When I don't reply, he gets down on his knees and raises his hands toward the heavens. "Praise God. It's a miracle."

I think about kicking him in the ribs, but in the end I just ignore him and walk to the door.

"Wait. Where are you go—" he begins, but by then I've slammed the door.

I walk on the right side of 201 until I'm directly across from the Outfitters, then cut across the highway quickly. That way, I avoid the sound of the river. If I hear those voices, I might get cold feet. And I need to do this. I need to put an end to the questions.

I know it's completely ridiculous. I know I'm going crazy and seeing people who aren't real. But they *feel* real, as real as Justin or Angela or anyone. And even though she can't be over there, even though it's impossible, I need to see. I need to prove to myself that all of this—Jack, Trey, my mother—is all in my head.

In the Outfitters, it's quiet because the buses have already departed for the day. There's a rather large older man there in red flannel and an L.L.Bean cap, reading a hunting magazine. I clear my throat. He looks up, startled. "Hi!" I say brightly. "I, um, saw an interesting graveyard on the other bank and I was wondering if there was a way I could get across to see it?"

He says yes with the first Down East Maine accent I've heard in a long time: "Ayuh." Most people in southern Maine now are from away and don't talk like that, which is a shame because I kind of like it. "You looking to rent a kayak?"

I bite my lip. "Well . . . if there's any way to stay out of the water, I'd prefer that."

All the while, his eyes are narrowed to tiny creases. Then he says, "Yeh the Ice Guhl!"

"Um, well . . ."

"Imagine that, the Ice Guhl wants to stay out of the riveh. What, the riveh got yeh good?" He's all animated, suddenly. "Well, theh a footbridge 'bout sixteen miles upstream. At put-in. Yeh have to get down the logging roads. Gets hahd cause theh not mocked."

I think for a second before I realize he's saying "marked." The roads are not marked. Great.

"Oh," I sigh. Justin and Angela have taken Monster to get

to the trailhead. Not that I would have taken it without asking him. He wouldn't have minded, but with my luck, since it's mud season, I probably would end up stuck on a remote logging road, never to be found again.

"That kayak soundin' betta and betta each minute, eh?" he asks. "I'd take yeh, but I'm right out straight heh."

I don't know what that means, but it sounds painful.

"Yeh can still rent on a thuty," he says.

I just stare. He writes something on a piece of paper and pushes it over the counter to me. It says *$30.*

"Cash only," he says. "Dough know howah wahk those credit cah thingies."

"Is it rough? Is it hard to get across from here?" I ask, my voice rising an octave.

"Nah. Buh yeh gah to make shaw yeh get theh befuh yeh reach the Kennebec. Gets a little hahd thah."

I dig into my pockets for the money but stop. The feeling of dread—being on the water—washes over me. I can't do it. As much as I want to see what's over there, I can't. "Isn't there anyone else who could take me?" I ask.

He shakes his head, just as a voice calls out behind me, "I can." I whirl around and Hugo is standing there, already holding a kayak paddle and grinning. He looks at the old man behind the counter and, in this most atrocious combination of Down East Maine and British Cockney, says, "It's wicked calm, taint that right, govnah?"

I don't care if he's going to help me. I still have to smack him.

CHAPTER FIFTEEN

Hugo suddenly transforms into Mr. Athletic as he takes the kayak and fastens on his life vest.

"Do you really know how to kayak?" I ask, skeptical, as I pull a vest over my jacket and fasten the strap of the helmet under my chin.

He snorts. "Well, let's just say I have more experience than you."

I glare at him.

"I've been kayaking since I was nine," he mutters. "Get in the boat. And don't do anything stupid like falling out, okay? Keep your arms and legs inside the kayak at all times. And enjoy your ride." The last part sounds like he's a flight attendant.

I get in. The kayak is even mushier and more unbalanced than the raft. A few prickles at the back of my neck seem to be telling me to turn around, go to the cabin, and watch *What Not to Wear*. But it's nothing too alarming. I can do this. I need to do this.

"What, exactly, about old cemeteries sounds good to you?" he asks as he sits in front of me.

"I don't know. I like the history, I guess," I say, which is the truth. When I was in third grade, we went on a class trip to Boston and I spent most of that time walking around the Granary Burying Ground. Most of the class went to the harbor, but my father asked the teacher to make an exception for me, because I was "afraid of the water." And back then, I was, because my father had told me so many horror stories about it—that drownings happened all the time, that there were creatures with tentacles that could pull you under, et cetera. So I spent three hours hanging out with Sam Adams and John Hancock and a bunch of other dead people. It was interesting, but I was disappointed when the rest of my class showed up and not one of them had been maimed by an octopus.

Hugo nods and pats his camera bag. "I do, too. Wanted to go across. Thought I could take some pictures. Guess that means we have something in common, huh?"

I snort. The horror.

We push off and immediately follow the flow, but then Hugo begins to paddle. He does a good job of keeping up with the current at first, and even I'm impressed. I never figured that the spindle-limbed guy would have much athletic ability. Soon we're halfway across, in the middle of the river. Hugo groans. His rhythmic motion falters a little, and he loses his grip and slows for a second. We begin to slide downstream.

"Keep going," I call to him. "We don't want to—"

He picks it up again. He mutters something like "I am" and some random curse word, which I'm sure is meant for me. I deserve it; I'm not helping at all, just calling out commands like a total backseat driver. I try to bite my tongue and let him do it, but then he stops again and we're slipping farther downstream.

I can't help it. I say, "Watch it, we're—"

"I know!" he erupts. "Shut it, Miss Life-is-but-a-dream-and-death-is-the-awakening."

I straighten. So, while looking for the Absolut, he found my book of private ramblings. What else did he find? "You went through my things? You disgusting creep!" I grab my paddle and nudge it into his spine.

"Ow, you bitch!" he snarls, and it must have been such a surprise because his own paddle slips from his grasp. He leans over and collects it before it can float away with the river. Though I have a great weapon, I guess this isn't the time to use it on him for being such a complete and utter scumbag. Because now the current is pushing us back toward the east bank. I tighten my grip on the paddle, but when I look up, I hear something, partially drowned out by the helmet over my ears and the rushing water.

Whispering.

Oh no.

I look around. There is nothing on the west bank. I turn, scanning the dark water, and finally focus on the east bank. Trey is there. He is cupping his hands around his mouth and yelling something, but the whispers have grown to a deafening buzz.

By now we've slipped so far down the river that I can no longer see the Outfitters or the cemetery. I fumble to get my paddle into position, but my hands are wet with perspiration and it falls out of my grip, splashing into the water. "Crap!" I yell. A lost paddle is twenty bucks. I reach down to get it and wrap my hand around the cold metal pole. But when I try to pull it back up, *it pulls me*. And then I can feel it moving.

It's not the paddle after all. It's a hand.

And all at once I know what Trey is shouting. He's shouting that I'm a complete idiot for not listening. He's shouting that I should have left when I had the chance.

The hand wraps around my wrist, tightening. Hugo has his back to me now, and he's fighting to keep the kayak upright, but it's tilting toward the water. The pressure is too much. I know I'm going, because before the hand yanks me over, the water is once again whispering its welcome. And I know that what happened before wasn't a freak accident. Things like this don't happen twice by mistake. Maybe I belong here, among the waves.

I'm not sure how much time passes. It feels like just a blink of an eye. One moment, I'm bracing for the shock of the cold water, and the next, I'm lying on the ground, coughing and sputtering river water all over myself. I sit up and immediately bonk my head into something hard. When I say "Ouch!" someone choruses with me.

"Damn, girl, is this the thanks I get for saving your butt twice?"

I open my eyes. Trey is there, rubbing his forehead. I try to apologize but end up coughing up some gritty black water into my hand. Gross. I wipe it on my life vest and look around. We're back on the east bank, a little downstream from where I set off. I know this because I can see the dock and the green roof of the Outfitters in the distance. The kayak is nowhere in sight. I'll probably have to pay for it and the paddles we lost. After all, it's not Hugo's fault.

I sit bolt upright. "Oh no. Hugo!"

"Relax, kid. I took care of him. He's back at the cabin, sleeping. He probably won't remember much of this when he wakes up."

"How can you . . . I don't understand. . . ."

"Yeah, you *don't.* That much is clear. So now's my time to do some explaining, I guess." His tone is angry. He wrings out the lower hem of his old shirt, which is open to the waist, revealing his tan chest. He catches me looking and I blush.

He turns away and starts pacing the shoreline. There are thousands of jagged little rocks and pieces of debris on the edge of the river, but they don't seem to bother his bare feet. Well, of course not; he's not real. "I thought I told you to get. What the hell did you do that again for?"

"I want to see my mother."

Surprise dawns on his face. I expect him to tell me that I'm crazy, that she's dead and gone and that's the end of it.

Instead, he narrows his eyes. "You can't see your momma. It's impossible."

"But she's there? She's across the river?"

He looks away, then nods reluctantly.

"So what Jack said was true," I whisper.

"No. Look." He comes up really close to me and grabs my wrist. "What that piece of slime says to you is *always* wrong. Don't you ever listen to nothing he's got to say. Got it?"

I don't like the way he's pulling on my wrist, almost hard enough to dislocate it. He looks down at it and remorse dawns on his face as he slowly releases it, then rubs the red welt his fingers have left.

"I'm sorry, kid."

His fingers are rough and misshapen. There are sore-looking red circles there, popped blisters, and scabs all over his palms. I pull my hand away from him. "Are you a ghost, too?"

"I'm a guide," he says.

"A guide for what?"

"I took your momma across. You were a kid then, so you don't remember."

"Of course I remember. You don't think I remember my own mom dying?"

"Sorry, kid. Anyway, that was my job, taking her across. And it's my job to take you across, too. When you're ready. And you ain't ready."

I stare at him hard. "You . . . you . . ." And suddenly I remember it all. My little fishing spot on the river. I went out there every day during the summers. My mom bought me that expensive new pole for my seventh birthday, and she would pack lemonade for me in a blue cooler and tell me to bring home a shark. And then one day that boy showed up, that funny-talking kid. He said he was waiting on a girl. My mother died three weeks later, and I never went back to that fishing spot again. "That—that was you?"

"You remember me?"

"I remember you catching all the fish in the river and letting them go. I was so angry." And then a realization hits me. "You . . . guided my mother? To where?"

"Across the river. To the place of the dead." He thunks on his temple as if to say *Where's my head?* "She—you—you are both river guardians. Royalty among the river dwellers. You probably didn't know that. She didn't know much about it, either, when I guided her."

"Wh-what?" I can't say anything more.

"The water is no place for final resting. It's always moving, too volatile. People who meet their deaths on or near the river need someone to guide them somewhere quiet, safe. Across the river. That's where you and your mother come in."

"And you? You are a guardian, too?"

He shakes his head. "My only job is to fetch the guardians and do what I can to protect them. I don't have your power. You have great magical powers, Kiandra."

I raise my eyebrows. "Like what?"

He chuckles. "Kiandra, you have no idea what you can do."

I just sit there, numb. The idea is crazy. It's crazy enough to be seeing these ghosts, but that my mother and I could have powers, could be tied to the water in that way? Nuts. "I think you have the wrong person. I do not have powers. I can't even put on a wet suit. And I nearly drowned in the river. *Twice*," I say, but all the while I'm thinking about my visions. About how my mother always loved the water so much, and how her skin was always clammy and smelled damp. How when she finally disappeared into the river forever, despite the horror of that event, a small part of me said, *Well, of course she did.*

He comes in close and sits on the bank next to me. He smells like pine needles and something spicy-sweet. "Do you need me to prove it to you?"

I nod. "That would be nice, since it's kind of impossible to believe."

"You didn't have to rent a kayak to go across the river, kid," he says.

"What? Are you saying I can part the waters? Or walk on water?" I joke.

He smiles. "Which would you prefer?"

My jaw drops. "I was only kidding."

But his face never changes. I get the suspicion that he's serious. "But you don't want to go over there," he says. "If you're over there, you ain't alive. And I'm trying to keep you alive. So don't try to go over there again, okay?"

"If I have such control over water, then why did you have to save me from drowning twice?"

"Because you don't know how to use your abilities, kid. Until you do, you can't protect yourself from nothing," he says, shaking his head. "You are Mistress of the Waters. That's no small thing."

"Mistress of the Waters?" I say the words, tasting them.

"Yeah." Then he mutters, "Pretty much the sorriest Mistress of the Waters I've ever come across."

I cross my arms. "What's that supposed to mean?"

"I've brought dozens of your ancestors across. But you are . . . different. I'm not supposed to take you across. Not yet. But damned if you're not giving me the hardest time keeping you out of trouble. You don't listen. You didn't listen when I told you that fancy pole of yours wouldn't catch you nothing, and you don't listen now."

I snort. Am I really being lectured by a ghost about how to live my life? "Jack told me *he* was sent to take me across."

"No," he says, his face stone. "Jack is no good. He's lying to you, trying to trick you."

"I don't understand. What does he want from me?"

He's not looking at me anymore. He's scanning the riverbank. I don't think he heard my question. He reaches down and grabs my wrist. "Look. We're not safe here. Can we go somewhere?"

"You can come back to the cabin with me."

He hesitates. "Can you see the river from there?"

I nod.

"I think I can do that. Can't get too far from the river."

"Or what?"

"Or I get pulled back. The river's like a stake in the ground with a chain tied to it. And I'm the dog." He reaches down and helps me stand. "Can you walk good? How's that ankle of yours?"

"It's not too bad," I say, putting my weight on it. I hop up and down. It's just a numb ache, barely perceptible. I move it back and forth, testing it, but then suddenly I must do the wrong thing, because pain shoots up my leg. I shriek and fall to my knees. "Except when I do that."

He reaches down and touches it. I feel the rough skin on his finger pad just barely swiping under my anklebone, and the whole thing begins to tingle. "Better?"

I jump. I move. I do everything I did before, but the pain does not come back. "So you did do it, last time? To my back? You can heal me?"

He nods like it's no big deal, and we start to walk toward the cabin. He's looking over his shoulder. Something is bothering him. As I walk behind him, I notice he is leaving a trail of small droplets of black blood on the dirt. I rush to keep up with him, and though he's holding his arm close to his chest, I know it's that same cut that's bleeding. It looks as fresh as ever. I pull off my jacket and clamp it over the thing. He doesn't argue. "Old war wound or not, I'm not letting you bleed all over the cabin."

"Thank you," he says softly.

"You're Trey Vance, aren't you?" I ask him, finally. "The boy who told on those other boys who killed the girl. I heard your story. They pulled a knife on you. That's where you got that cut. And you jumped in the water but you couldn't swim."

He laughs, but there's sadness in his voice. "That's what

happens over time. Stories get twisted out of shape. But no. I couldn't swim. Lived my whole life by water, first in New York and then in Oklahoma, and never learned to swim. How's that for irony? The one at my home outside of Tulsa was muddy and full of them leeches. No fun. Some kids on the river where I died even made a rhyme up about it after, as a warning.

"Trey Vance, who took a chance
And was pushed in the river grim.
He lost his life not by a knife
But because he couldn't swim.

"They say I'm famous in twelve counties. Whenever kids don't want to learn to swim, their mommas always say, 'Now, little Bobby, you know what happened to Trey Vance, don't you? Get your butt back in the water.'"

"Thought you said you were a 'powerful good swimmer'?"

He nods. "That's the good thing about this place. You get to be what you wanted most to be when you died. And hell, if I'd have been a good swimmer, I'd still be alive."

I look down at his arm, which he's hugging to his body. "You can heal me, but you can't heal yourself?"

He shrugs. "That power's beyond me."

"Is it beyond the all-powerful Mistress of the Waters?"

"You joke about it, but that's 'cause you don't understand it," he says. We cross the highway and start up the driveway.

"Can't heal the dead. But *you* can bring a person back to life. The Mistress of the Waters can do that. It'll damn near destroy all her power, but she can do it. I think that's what they want your momma for."

"Who wants her?" I sputter.

"They want her to make them alive again."

"Who?"

"Don't know. Jack, I think." His face twists. "It's hard to get you to understand, when even I don't know what's what, sometimes."

I groan. "I *want* to understand it, but you're making it so damn hard. If I'm destined to become this royal-over-the-waters, shouldn't I just go and accept my destiny?"

"No. Not now." He stops suddenly, trying to think of the words, then exhales, defeated. "Being here is dangerous. Too dangerous for you."

"Why? Is it because of Jack? Who sent you, anyway?"

"Mistress Nia," he says softly. "Your momma."

Every time someone says my mother's name, I cringe inside. I'm so used to having that reaction to her, I can't rid myself of it. And so when Trey says her name again, I bite down hard on my tongue and don't say a word until we're in the cabin. When I open the door, I can already hear loud snores emanating from one of the upstairs bedrooms. Hugo, no doubt. Our little kayak trip seems a million years away, almost as if it never happened. And the funny thing is, when I look down, I realize my clothes are completely dry. Not like they dried, but like they were never wet in the first place. They're not stiff with river grime. My hair even smells like the shampoo I used the evening before.

I turn to Trey, about to ask him why my mother would send him as a warning, when I see him staring into the hallway mirror. There's no reflection. I am standing behind him and yet all I see in the glass is myself. He shakes his head. "I ain't seen myself in a mess of years. What year is it now? 1940? 1945?"

I know my eyes are bulging. "What year did you . . ."

He chews on his lower lip. "Last I was like you, it was 1935."

How could he have somehow misplaced so many years? "It's much later," I say.

He grimaces. "It's hard keeping track of the days here. I tried for a while but lost it." He runs his hands through his hair. "What do I look like now? Hell?"

"Um . . . fine," I say. For someone who has been dead for so many decades, he doesn't look half bad.

He looks around the house and whistles long and loud. "This the way people living these days? This a hotel?"

"No, it's Angela's parents' vacation cabin."

He raises his eyebrows. "Just the three of them? Live here?"

I nod. "But only a couple weeks out of the year."

"Dang, I was born at the wrong time." He walks into the kitchen and opens the freezer. "Heh. If this ain't one of them—what are they called? Refrigerators. We had one. Brand-new. My dad got it for my momma for her birthday."

He turns the under-the-counter can opener on and steps

backward in a hurry when it begins to whir. I help him shut it off. "That opens cans."

"Angry little thing, ain't it?" He shakes his head at it like it's a naughty puppy and begins playing with some of the other appliances. I explain each one to him, and each time, he laughs and shakes his head. Then he turns to the microwave. "What's this? This chew the food for you?"

He doesn't wait for an answer. His eyes fasten on the fake moose antlers over the fireplace. He whistles again. "Must've took ten men to bring that beast down, heh?"

I don't want to tell him they're fake. Based on the way he reacted to everything in the kitchen, he already knows the people of today are a bunch of wusses who can't do anything for themselves. "Um, I guess."

There's a noise in the foyer, probably just the house settling, but it reminds me that Angela and Justin might come home at any minute, or Hugo might wake up. Trey has moved on to the bookcase. "Hey, I had that one, too. *Journey to the Centre of the Earth.* My momma bought it for me on my seventeenth birthday. Never finished it, though. Died before I could."

He says it so matter-of-factly, it makes me gasp. "You can borrow it, if you want," I say, since I doubt that any of us will be doing any real reading this weekend.

"Yeah?" He gets all excited, like I offered him a Porsche, and takes the book down from the shelf. He stares at it for a minute, and then gently puts it back. "I'd best not. Don't want to muss it up."

"Um, I'm afraid you can't stay here. My friends will be back any minute," I say.

"They can't see me, kid."

"Yeah, but I can. I can't act normal if you're around."

He nods. "All right, all right. But knowing your momma wanted me to protect you, ain't that enough for you to get yourself home?"

I shake my head. "I don't know who to believe. Jack is telling me one thing. You're telling me something else. All of it is so unbelievable. And I know I should be running in the other direction, but I can't leave until I know. If my mother is here, I want to see her."

He throws his hands up in frustration. I'm clearly getting on his nerves. "I told you. That ain't possible. Across the river is her kingdom. She can't abandon it. You can't see her unless you cross the river. And you need to be dead for that. If you cross, you ain't coming back. And you like your life, don't you? You don't want to leave it?"

"I do, but—"

"There's another part to this story. Listen," he says, his face turning to stone. "According to your momma, there's a relation of yours from many years ago. This person would have inherited the title, but died very young, and has been living on the outskirts of your momma's kingdom, in the shadows. The story is that ever since this person came here, they've been wanting to step in. They've been off in secret, developing these powers. This person's been in this kingdom a long time, longer than your momma's been ruling, and they're awful strong. Stronger than your momma. Stronger than you, because not only was this person destined to rule, but they know more about your powers than anyone. And they're angry. Real angry at your momma."

I swallow. "I don't understand. Who is this person? Jack?"

"Doesn't matter. All it means is that you need to get."

"Can't my mother just come to the edge? Just so I can . . ." I trail off. This is so stupid. Asking to see my mother. My mother, who abandoned me. She's dead. Gone. Even if I could see her, I shouldn't want to.

"It doesn't work like that, kid."

I exhale. "Of course it doesn't. Can you tell me something? When you die, do you stay here forever?"

"No. Everything fades. From the moment you were brought into the world, you were dying. How fast you do that is up to a lot of things. I've been here more years than I can count. But I guess it's good to know that when things end, you can start again."

I blink, fighting back the memory of my mother, sitting on the edge of my bed, telling me something so similar. *Sometimes things end. And it's comforting to be able to begin again.*

He wags a finger at me. "But listen, girl. Stop getting ideas. If anything happens to you, your momma'll skin me. Not alive, because that ain't possible, but you get the picture. You're all she ever talks about."

"I—I am?" I sputter. I can't believe that's true. He must have me confused with someone else's daughter. Anyway, it doesn't matter. "I can't leave. Not when I know my mother is over there." I bite my lip, thinking of my mother. She left me; why wouldn't I do the same to her? But the answer is immediate: I'm not like her. "I don't abandon my family."

Now he starts to pace around me, hands on hips. When he stops, his eyes burn into me. He's angry. "If anyone could be the death of me, you're it. You can't do nothing about it, kid. Accept it. Just do what your momma said."

I start to argue with him, but then I hear something. We both freeze at the sound of tires on gravel, coming nearer, up the driveway.

He reaches out and at first I think he's going to poke me, but instead, he gently touches my cheek with his icy finger, leaving a line of tingles there. I wonder if it tingles that way because he's not human or for another reason, but already I yearn to feel it again. I want to grab his hand and keep it there, but before I can, he says, "Go home."

And then it's like he was never there at all.

CHAPTER SIXTEEN

When Angela and Justin return, they look tired, not exhilarated, like I expect them to. They live for hiking and outdoors stuff, and yet Angela just collapses on the sofa without so much as a nod in my direction. Justin drops their backpacks on the foyer floor and studies me, an unfocused, confused look on his face. Finally, it's like something switches on in his brain, because he says, "You feeling better?"

I'm standing in the kitchen, which is probably not something I should be doing if I just sprained my ankle. I start to limp over to him. "Well, uh—"

"You have your hiking boots on. Did you go outside?" He sounds suspicious, which catches me off guard. Justin is not the suspicious type.

"Yeah, I—I wanted to get some fresh air, so I just went out for a little bit," I lie. "How was your hike?"

He kisses the top of my head. "Cool. Would have been more fun with you there, though."

I smile at him. Of course he's just saying that.

"I'm going to catch a shower at the Outfitters. Then we can go see that movie, okay?"

"Sounds good," I say. A movie is the last thing on my mind, though. I can't stop thinking of what Trey said. Someone is conspiring to overthrow the Mistress. *My mother, the Mistress.* This woman, the most important person of my childhood, who I adored beyond words, is only yards away. As incredible as that sounds, after all I've witnessed, I believe it. Inexplicably, I can almost feel her presence. It is what drew me to this place. Suddenly I realize why I haven't been able to leave. Here, I'm enveloped by that clammy yet comforting feeling I used to get whenever she touched me. *I belong here.* I know now that my mother felt the same.

My mother. Even just thinking about her now, when I haven't in so long, ties my stomach in knots. Trey said I'm all she ever talks about. And here, all this time, I've never talked about her. I pushed her out of my mind and off my tongue for so long, I can barely think the word without clenching my jaw. *Mother.*

I go upstairs into the bedroom where I left my bag and begin to change. Though there is no trace of grit on my skin or dampness anywhere from my plunge in the Dead, my clothes just feel wrong. They scratch at my skin almost as if they were full of river. The sun is beginning to set, casting orange streaks on the river across the way. I watch it as I kick off my mud-crusted boots and peel my shirt and jeans off.

I stand there in my bra and panties, rifling through my bag, looking for my lip gloss. I never go anywhere without slathering my lips in the stuff. When I find it, I step to the mirror and smudge the bubble-gum-pink color into my lips. Then I find my brush and run it through my hair, letting the hair fall loose down my back. I stand back to look at myself. Two days away from civilization, and I still look presentable. Awesome. I'm about to reach down and find my shirt when I see it.

A face among the dark trees outside.

I gasp and turn, reaching for clothes, and that's when I make out the figure that is standing there, watching me. Jack. He knows I see him, and yet he doesn't shy away. He doesn't move, almost as if he is a part of the landscape. He keeps staring at me, this look—of approval? No, of *wanting*—on his face. His eyes are full of fire, so full I'm suddenly aware of this burning sensation that starts in my chest and radiates down between my legs.

What is wrong with me? From what Trey said, I should know Jack is bad. Trey said he's the enemy. Still, I can't help thinking that there's something about him I want so deeply. I drop the shirt to the floor, only because I know it would please him. I want to please him. I want it with everything I am. My fingers are not my own; they feel like they are attached to puppet strings as they reach behind my back and undo the clasp of my bra.

There's a faint noise in the hallway. I whirl around to see that the door is open an inch. It shudders a little, and that's when I see an eye in the opening. Refastening my bra, I recognize it just as the door opens fully and Hugo steps into the room, hitting me with a wave of foul-smelling air, a mixture of old alcohol, vomit, and morning breath. He hasn't even cleaned himself up; he has the worst five o'clock shadow and his hair is sticking up straight at the very top, kind of like a Mohawk. Gagging, I grab my shirt and hold it over my chest as he drawls, "Hey, you."

"What are you doing in here?" I shout. "Get out of here!"

He's running his tongue around his mouth like it's his toothbrush. He eyes me like he's got something on me. "Why were you . . . Who was out there?"

I turn back to the window. Jack is gone. In that instant, everything I was doing just seems so stupid. What *was* I doing? I'm starting to blush, something I don't want Hugo to see, or else he'll know. He'll know he's gotten to me. So I grab my hairbrush and hurl it at him. "Get out!" I scream.

He ducks away and it smacks against the wall near the door, leaving a crescent-shaped dent in the plaster. "Ice Girl my ass. More like Psycho Girl," he calls behind me.

Psycho Girl, I think, as I put on my new T-shirt and jeans, carefully looking out into the darkening forest every so often. But Jack never returns. Maybe he was never there in the first place. I'd hate for Hugo to be right, but this time, he probably is.

I'm lacing up my hiking boots when Angela comes into the room. Her hair is damp, so she must have showered. "Hi, Lucky Charms," she says. "How's your ankle?"

"Hi, um . . ." I think Angela spends most of her free time

trying to think of new cereals to call me, but this time, I'm blank. "Trix?" There's a cereal called that, right? "Much better."

She collapses on the bed next to me. "What're you up to?"

I blush deeper, thinking of what I was up to. I don't want to talk about it. So I say, "I'd rather find out what you were up to."

She sits up and her eyes widen. "What do you mean?"

"Last night. I saw you and Hugo getting cozy."

"Oh," she says. "Nothing. He's kind of annoying. And creepy."

I cringe, thinking of him watching me through the open door. But Angela . . . Angela doesn't think badly of anyone. "What makes you say that?"

"Well, he went through everyone's stuff to get the vodka. Who in their right mind would do something like that?"

"I know. He read my journal," I say, shuddering.

"Ew, he did? And he always seems to say the wrong thing. I just—he's not my type, you know?"

Finally, she comes to her senses! "So, what is your type?" I ask, but the thing is, I know. She tells me this all the time. Someone more like her. Someone more like . . . my boyfriend.

This time, though, she doesn't say it. She leans back and stares at the ceiling. She's unusually thoughtful. Maybe being in the wilderness unleashes her quiet, pensive side. Maybe she is at one with nature. Then she opens her mouth and the last thing I'd expected comes out. "Prom's tonight."

"It is?" For the past couple of days, I haven't thought of

myself in ice-blue satin at all, but it's always been in the back of my mind, despite all that has been going on.

She sits up and pinches my cheek like I'm three. "I know you wanted to go."

"I never said I wanted to," I say.

"You don't have to," she singsongs. "You've been one of my best friends for ten years. I know."

I shrug. "But this is . . ." I'm searching for a word, but every one I can think of to describe the time up here is negative. The longer I pause, the less real I sound. Finally, I choke out, "Fun, too."

She titters a little, back to the Angela I know and love. Still, there's something wrong with her behavior, but I can't tell what it is. She's so jumpy, like a spring, yet guarded. She's hiding something. She's terrible at keeping secrets, almost as bad as Justin. "Sure it is. Anyway, *The River Wild* is all they ever play up here. I've seen it a hundred times. You'd think they could play something different for once."

I shrug. "I've never seen it."

"Well, it's okay. But I just wanted to tell you, I think I'm staying in."

Okay, there's *definitely* something going on. Angela loves darkened movie theaters and big containers of popcorn. I raise my eyebrows. "You're staying in? With Hugo?"

"Ew. He refuses to shower even though he smells," she groans. "There's a zombie movie marathon on tonight and a can of SpaghettiOs with my name on it in the pantry. I'll be fine."

"Okay," I venture, studying her closely as if her expression will reveal something. But it doesn't. She just smiles and tries to grab my cheek again, but I swat her hand away before she can.

"Have fun," she says, leaving me alone.

I walk downstairs, hoping to avoid Hugo. Justin is standing in the living room, digging into the pockets of his oversized sweatshirt. There's something in there, because I can see his fingers playing with it, but I can't tell what. He has his Red Sox cap turned backward, which makes him look like an innocent little boy, but something about his expression is wrong. Justin can never hide anything; his face always gives him away. "What?" I ask when I'm standing in front of him.

He brings one corner of his mouth up in a smile. "Nothing. Let's go."

He grabs my hand and we walk out into the night. By now it's dark, with charcoal-colored clouds obscuring the moon. An owl hoots in the distance and the river hums along, but it's almost as if we've walked into a closet. I can't see a thing. I cling to Justin, shivering. I know the dead probably won't come to me with him around, but at the same time, I don't want to test it. Justin leads the way, and in another couple of minutes I can see the orange light spilling from the Outfitters. There are no people outside, though, and the barbecue pit is empty. It looks kind of deserted. "Do a lot of people watch the movie?" I ask.

He shrugs. "Some."

His voice is so cool, so aloof, that it startles me. I stop in my tracks before we cross the highway. "What is going on with you?"

He won't look me in the eye. He just hitches his shoulders again. "Nothing. Come on. Let's go."

He doesn't wait for me; he starts jogging so that I'm trailing two steps behind him. We cross the highway and find the path toward the Outfitters. When we're near the door, I inspect the wipe-off board that talks about the daily activities. It says:

TODAY the RIVER is at 7,500 CFS
Dinner at 6 p.m. will be franks and burgers
Be SAFE out THERE!
Thank You for Choosing Northeast Outfitters

But nowhere at all does it say that tonight is Movie Night on the terrace. I'm about to ask Justin how he knows that there'll be a movie when I've never seen it posted anywhere, when he turns to me and reaches into his pocket. He pulls out this kind of crushed, but still very pretty, red rose, surrounded by a little baby's breath. The petals are black and wilting around the edges, and some of them fall off in his hands. "Crap," he mutters.

I stare at it, openmouthed. "What is that?"

He lets the loose petals fall to the ground and holds it up for me. "It used to be a flower. I think."

I just stare at it. "It's a corsage? For, like, prom? Where did you—"

He nods. "I bought it Wednesday."

"I don't get it," I say as I take it from him and affix it to my shirt. I look kind of silly wearing a corsage on this ensemble, especially since we're just going to watch a movie. He opens the door to the Outfitters, and when I walk in, Spiffy is giving Justin the eye. They communicate soundlessly, and I do a tennis match head-swivel to see what each of them is trying to say, but it's just raised eyebrows, winks, and nods.

"This way," Justin says, pulling me into a room. A sign on the door says it's the KENNEBEC ROOM, which I think must be on the way to the terrace. It's dark inside, like a movie theater.

But suddenly a speaker begins to crackle, and music begins to pour out of it. It's some cheesy slow song I've never heard before. Disco lights begin to flash white circles around the room. I strain in the dizzying moving pattern of darkness and light but don't see a movie screen or chairs. It's just a big, empty room with lacquered wood floors, like a gymnasium. In the corner is a banner, painted with big black lettering: WAYVIEW HIGH SCHOOL SENIOR PROM. I turn to Justin. He's looking at it, scratching his head, which is what he always does when he's embarrassed. "Justin, what is going on?" I ask.

His shoulders sag. "This was way better in my mind."

"No, it's . . . nice!" I say brightly, relieved.

So this is why he was acting so strange. He never could keep secrets from me. Justin is just too simple, too honest for something like that. I'm relieved it wasn't anything bad, like . . . well, I don't know what.

"You said you didn't care about prom, but I know you did," he says softly. "You're a good person for going along with us. And I know it's missing all the best things about being at prom, like getting all dressed up and seeing all your friends, but—"

I smile and pull him to the center of the room. I draw him to me, lean my head against his chest so I can hear the thumping of his heart, and we begin to sway. "You're wrong," I whisper into his neck. "The best thing about prom would be going with you, the best boyfriend in the world."

I close my eyes to lose myself in the music, but he's stopped moving. He's standing there, stiff. I pull away and look into his eyes. The lights flash in rhythm on the deep ridges of his frown. And I know there is something else.

He will not look me in the eye; instead, his focus is somewhere over my head. He opens his mouth to speak. At first nothing comes out. Then finally the words come. "I kissed her. I kissed Angela."

My breath hitches. "What?"

He doesn't repeat it. He doesn't have to, and I don't want him to. I heard him perfectly the first time, and I don't want those words scraping my eardrums again. But I just don't want to believe it. He swallows. "It was a mistake. It meant nothing."

I shake my head. "Kisses *always* mean something," I say softly.

"Well, this one didn't mean anything. Really," he says. "We

came back from the hike and we were setting up the streamers here, and . . ."

He keeps speaking but I'm not really listening because I'm looking at the streamers. I didn't notice them before, but the entire room is decked out in our school colors, with bright red and yellow streamers everywhere. Angela helped him with this. It must have taken hours. I realize that he kissed her here. Right where we're standing. Something thick is building in the back of my throat, making it hard to swallow, hard even to breathe. My boyfriend. And my best friend.

"And we were just joking around, dancing, and I lost my mind for a second because the next thing I knew I was kissing her. It's not Ange's fault. It's mine. It was just . . ."

He says "stupid" at the same time I say "what you've always wanted."

I don't know why I say it, maybe because, deep down, I've always thought that. He's shaking his head, only shaking his head, back and forth, like some stupid dog trying to dry its fur. Maybe if he'd say the word, actually say "No, never, I never wanted that, God, Ki, it's you I've always loved," maybe if he fell to my feet and covered the room with apologies, I could believe him. But he's just standing there, shaking his head, mute. I fight back the tears with everything I can but they're spilling over my cheeks as he grabs me by my elbows, pulling me toward him. I rip myself away from him and shove against his chest as hard as I can. Usually it's like trying to move a mountain, but this time, he steps backward, stricken.

I tear the corsage off my T-shirt, not paying attention to the hole that it leaves in the fabric, revealing my lacy black bra. He's still standing there, frozen. He opens his mouth to speak, but again no words come out. *Why does he have no words for me? He's supposed to know me better than anyone! We're supposed to be able to talk about things!* I hurl the corsage at him and fly out the door, into the cold air, down to the river.

"Trey!" I scream into the blue night. "Trey! I'm ready! Take me across."

The wind picks up and the tips of the tall pines are swaying, almost bowing to me. Bowing to the newest Mistress of the Waters. Because that is what I was destined to be. And right now, that is what I want to become. I race through blackness, unsure if I'm headed toward the river, but the rocky embankment is growing steeper and steeper as my legs fly beneath me. Too fast. Soon I am sliding, and as I reach out to steady myself the toe of my boot slams against something hard, sending me stumbling forward. All at once I am flying through the air. The last thing I remember is the crushing pain in my chest, and maybe, probably, it's the breaking of my heart.

CHAPTER SEVENTEEN

My nightmares are worse than they have ever been. Justin and Angela, walking away from me as I slide down the muddy embankment toward the river. I'm screaming for help, but they are too enamored of one another to hear me. I claw at the earth, but my fingers just rake through mud. The girl in the pink party dress is standing over me. She spews more mud from her mouth, then reaches toward me. At first I think she is going to help me. Instead, she entwines her fingers in the hair at the top of my head and pushes my face into the soft earth. I can't breathe; all I can do is taste the thick, gritty stuff as it spreads into my mouth and nostrils. Now even screaming isn't possible. Someone is chanting something. *You're a stupid girl,* a female voice whispers in my ear. *Stupid, stupid.*

My throat is so dry it burns, which is ironic considering the background noise is the rushing water, so close I can probably touch it. I smell tree sap. Wisps of hair fly in my face, tickling me. I try to sweep them away with my hand, but I can't lift my arm. I take inventory and realize I can't lift either arm, or my legs. My limbs ache numbly, as if they're bound so tightly that my feet and hands tingle. I'm afraid to open my eyes, because I know that what I'll see won't be good.

When I will my eyes open, it's so dark that all I see are the faint outlines of the pine trees. I twist my head either way, looking for the source of the voice. Was it just my imagination again? Have I been left here to die, alone, at the base of this tree?

Then I hear footsteps. A face shockingly pale and ghost-like appears just inches from mine. The voice is the same as the one I heard in my dream. "She's awake! Get her some water."

My eyes ache as I try to open them, as if the lids are weighted down. When I force them open, I see only black-ness. Water should be the last thing I need, but when a cup reaches my lips I lap at it savagely, like a dog, feeling it spill down my chin and into my throat. It's strangely thick and oily and smells of mold and earth, but I don't care. I swallow and the pain subsides, and when I open my eyes again, things come into focus.

I stare at her. Everything about her is familiar. It's Lan-nie. My imaginary best friend from long ago. She holds up a lantern between us to look into my eyes. Hers are pretty and round, like pearls, with concern. She's not imaginary. She's real.

"Lannie?" I ask, struggling to rise. "What are you—"

She pushes me down and gently relaxes me on a bed of pine needles. "Shhh. You should rest."

"Well, who do we have here?" a male voice calls from a distance. I strain in the darkness and see him sauntering toward me. Jack. Immediately I catch my breath, and despite the pain everywhere in my body, I feel warm. Despite all the warnings Trey gave me, I know I am blushing. Why does Jack do this to me?

He gives me a seductive half smile, like he knows what I'm thinking. I look away, at Lannie, in time to see her glare at him. Jack, all six-feet-and-change of him, seems to fold in under the stare of the barely five-foot girl. He lowers his head and silently steps back.

I begin to sit up. "I need to go home. I need to—" Suddenly I remember dancing with Justin under the disco lights at the Outfitters. The expression on his face. His confession reverberates in my ears. *I kissed Angela.* I can't go back to him. I don't want to see him now, and maybe not ever. I slump back to the ground.

Jack steps closer to me. This near, his eyes threaten to set me afire, so I look away, to his knees. He whispers, "Can I get you anything?"

My heart skips at his words, as if he has offered me the world. I think about what Trey said. About Jack being the enemy. About how nothing Jack tells me is true. And so a small part of me wants to push him away, say no thank you, and be on my way. But the larger part of me is screaming,

Get closer! It's not that I've forgotten how to say no. It's just that with Jack, the word has ceased to exist in my vocabulary. I find myself nodding in agreement, whispering, "Anything."

He laughs, breaking me out of my trance. *Whoa. I'm a total goofball. What is happening to me?*

"Something to eat?" He holds out a granola bar, the kind they sell at the Outfitters. "Now you cannot accuse me of ignoring the unique needs of the living."

I take the bar from him. It's crushed like a pancake but I hold it like it's a precious gem. Lannie watches us intently, her expression lost between amusement and questioning. She sweeps her dark, pretty hair over her shoulder and scratches her neck. For the first time I see there are horrible bruises there, as if someone choked her. I recall how we used to play hide-and-seek on the river in New Jersey, and how I'd run in and out among the trees, lost and confused, only to find her hanging from a tree by her neck. She always did things like that, shocking things. She said it was only in fun, because everything else was so boring. I start to say something, but she notices me looking and brings her hair forward quickly and anxiously, concealing the bruises once more.

A little girl steps out from among the trees, smoothing the skirt of her pink party dress, despite the fact that it's covered in mud. As is her entire chin. Mud is oozing from her mouth. She's staring at me curiously. When she is only an arm's length away, she stoops, reaches out, and tugs on a lock of my hair. She pulls again and again, like she's ringing a bell, her head tilted in question. Her expression, inquisitive yet forlorn, does not change.

"Um, hi," I say to her.

Jack looks at her and rolls his eyes. He explains, "Vi doesn't talk. She's Lannie's sister."

Lannie puts a protective arm around her sister and begins to massage her small shoulder as the three of them beam at me like I'm a long-lost relative, here for a visit. "It's so nice to have you here," Lannie says. "I've missed you, Kiandra. I've missed our talks. Where have you been all this time?"

I nod. I've missed her, too. Even though I only saw her in the visions I had during those two years I lived on the river, I feel close to her, like she grew up with me. Actually, no, she was always older, always more mature, and she never changed. Her hair was always long, and chestnut brown, and she was never in anything other than that white dress. From what I remember, the last time we'd talked, it was about normal seven-year-old things. She liked tubing, fishing, and hopscotch, and all the things I liked, yet she always looked older. "My mother died, and we moved away," I say.

She makes a *tsk-tsk* noise. "Shame. But you know your mother is here, yes?"

I nod. "So I've heard."

"You were very fond of her?"

I shrug. "I was seven. Seven-year-old girls are always fond of their mothers, aren't they?"

"I suppose. But now you're not?"

"I don't know her anymore," I sigh. "She left me. To come here, I guess. I guess this place was more important to her than her family."

"I understand. So you don't want to see her, then?"

"I do," I say immediately. "But the one guy who's supposed to take me there is under orders not to."

"You mean Trey Vance?" she asks, pursing her lips. "That's shortsighted of your mother. Her powers are fading, but she denies it."

"They are?"

She laughs so unexpectedly and loudly that I throw back my head, banging it hard against the tree trunk behind me. She looks at Jack, who has been leaning against a tree trunk, examining his fingernails, but suddenly springs to attention when her eyes fall on him. Then she touches my hand. Her hand is so cold, clammy. Instantly I think of my mother. "Kiandra, we need you." She motions behind her. "Jack will explain things to you."

"Wait," I say as I realize what she is about to do. "Don't leave me with—"

I stop because, at the same time, I *want* to be left alone with him. She flings her hair over her shoulder and walks away until all I can see is her white dress, glowing in the pale blue light of the moon.

Jack comes toward me, and my heart starts thrumming as he does. He grins like he knows what he's doing to me. Like he relishes me going crazy for him. He touches my chin. His finger is surprisingly warm, and with that simple touch he sends electric shocks through my body. I know I'm quivering from head to toe. I know it's visible. My cheeks redden even more.

He sits down on the grass, cross-legged. "You're afraid of me?"

When my mouth opens, my teeth are chattering. I'm not afraid of him, but I know I should be. And *that's* what I'm afraid of. "Trey," I whisper. "He says you'll hurt me."

He leans forward. "I won't hurt you. Unless you want me to."

I stare at him.

He grins. "I'm joking. I am not out to hurt you."

"Why were you practically dragging me across the river this morning, then?"

"I was only helping. You're being lured to the water. You wanted to go across, but you're afraid. And you needn't be. Once you're over there, you'll see."

I eye him suspiciously. "You didn't have to drag me. Anyway, I thought it's Trey's job to take me across. Not yours."

He laughs. "And I'm not allowed to help the kingdom out?"

"You almost killed me," I mutter.

His face is grave, regretful. "Do not say that. I am not some kind of monster. Trey has good reason to hate me, though, I suppose. He's thinking of something that happened a long time ago."

"What happened a long time ago?"

"You've heard how he died, yes?" he asks. "Your friends told those horribly inaccurate ghost stories around the campfire a few nights ago. Were you listening?"

"How could I not? And I *saw* it, as it was happening. I saw him fall into the water. I saw him drown."

"Ah. Your powers allow you to see those things." He presses his lips together. "You didn't see who killed him, though."

"No, I couldn't see that. Two boys killed him, I think."

"Or so the story goes," he says with a shrug. "But the truth is, Trey was killed by only one person. And you're looking at him."

CHAPTER EIGHTEEN

My mind whirls with all the visions I've seen and fragments of the story Justin told. The blade slashing at Trey's arm. The cold water bubbling over his head. The desperate attempt to break the surface, to breathe. *That's the one. Get him.* "No. No," I say, "There were two. Someone told someone . . . to get—"

"I don't know what your visions are, but I assure you, I was there. I was the *only one* there."

I pull my knees to my chest and press myself against the tree trunk, as far away from him as I can get without leaving my position. "Trey was killed because he turned in a murderer. He saw a murder. Who else did you—"

He grabs my hand, immediately sending a chill up to my elbow. Only when my hand is in his do I realize how violently it has been shaking. He looks into my eyes and I feel dizzy and breathless from the weight of his stare. "I am not a monster. I do not like to talk about my time among the living. I squandered it. I made mistakes. Mistakes I wish I could undo. But I can't."

For some reason, I think of Justin. He'd said kissing Angela was a mistake, too. Back then, I didn't want to, *couldn't* believe that mistakes were possible. But though Jack's sin is so much more damnable, looking into his eyes, I am surprised at how easily I'd be willing to believe he has changed. "But you've changed?" I whisper, hoping that the answer is yes.

He doesn't have to say a thing. *I'm his servant.* As this thought flickers in my mind, it brings a moment of clarity. *Servant! What am I doing? What is wrong with—* But by then he is so near that I can feel the curve of his body pressing against mine, so cold that even though we are separated by clothing, his skin sears my flesh. He holds up my hand and presses his palm flat against mine, and all I can do is marvel at how perfectly and seamlessly they seem to go together. His face is so near to me that his breathing tickles my chin. "Sometimes we get caught in a whirlpool. No matter what we do to escape, we can't avoid being pulled under. Kiandra, I'm still in the whirlpool."

"You don't have to be. There's always a way out."

"Perhaps I haven't found it yet," he whispers, as though he's already dismissed the idea. His eyes are on my lips, which are waiting for him, trembling.

The thought of Justin flickers dimly in the back of my mind, a dying light among a thousand brilliant stars. I don't think I've ever wanted anything more than this, now. The anticipation is painful. "Kiss me," I murmur, and fully surrendering to my role as his own, I manage a "please" with the last of my breath.

He moves forward an almost imperceptible distance; then, in insult to my waiting mouth, his lips spread into a smile. He pulls away and stands. "If you don't want to help us, why don't you go back to the living? Why are you wasting our time?"

I open my eyes, momentarily bewildered and shamed. My mouth opens but words will not come out.

"If you want to help us, you need to go across," he snaps. "Now."

"I want . . . ," I begin, but I don't know what I want. Ten minutes ago, what I would have wanted was to be anywhere but with him. He frightened me. And yet something has changed, and now I want to help him. I want it more than anything. Now, having him here, so near, I realize that what's right for me and what simply *feels* right are two different things, and I can't trust myself to know the difference. Maybe I am in the whirlpool, too. He leans over me until his lips are once again right before mine. And then he does it, he kisses me. It's not like kissing Justin, not at all, because the taste of Jack is something foul, sour, like mold and rotten things, and still I push against him, my mouth moving against his, wanting more. I wrap my arms around him, pulling myself to him, lacing my fingers in his hair, every inch of me burning until I realize that my fingers are kneading through something wet and spongy, and that pieces of it are coming off in my hands.

I open my eyes and there is nothing there, only the quiet

outlines of the trees, still in the bright moonlight. I'm crouched on my hands and knees on the ground, in a puddle of mud. My hands and most of my arms are painted black with muddy leaves.

I'm not sure how I manage to get up and stumble through the woods, toward the cabin. I don't hear the sound of my feet hitting the ground. My breath billows in a cloud in front of me, and I blow through it. My hands feel sticky and wet and yet most of my body is numb, as if it has fallen into a deep sleep. Everything in the world seems asleep; there are no people, no sounds, not even the rush of the water I've come to expect. I stop for a moment and hold my hands in front of me. Yes, blood. So much blood. By now I can see the lights of the cabin. I rush across the highway, not bothering to stop. I must get home. I must get help.

I somehow get inside, and the heat is so intense my face feels like it's on fire. Justin is standing under the giant moose antlers, clutching his head in both hands like he's trying to lift it from his body. Angela is on the couch, chewing on her thumbnail, something she always does when she's nervous. I expect them to both react when they see me coming, but they don't. Justin continues to squeeze his head like his hands are a vise, and Angela stares off at the fireplace, even though there isn't a fire there. I'm about to shout for help when Justin throws down his arms.

"I am such an idiot. I screwed everything up," he says miserably.

"Oh, stop," Angela says.

"It's my fault she ran away. And now who knows what could happen to her? She's not thinking clear. I really screwed it up," he mumbles.

I stop for a moment, glad to hear him admit his guilt, then rush forward. "I'm here," I say, holding out my hands.

I expect them to turn toward me. I expect to see their faces contort in horror. I expect Angela to launch into Florence Nightingale mode, ushering me to the couch, and Justin to whip out his cell and call an ambulance. None of these things happens. Well, not at first. After a long pause, Justin reaches into the pocket of his cargo shorts and pulls out his phone. "I need to call," he says. But he's not looking at me.

I move forward, into the room. "Justin," I say to him.

But he won't look at me. I'm standing where I can reach out and touch Angela, and all she does is continue to study and chew on her fingernails, as if I'm not even there. As if . . .

I look down at the blood seeping through my jacket, making it look sleek and black, like a seal's skin. Then I stand between them. "Justin?"

Angela says, "Yeah. I think you need to."

Need to what? I turn to her, I'm standing right in front of her, and her eyes are on me, but they're not. They're focused on what's behind me. Justin. I move closer to her, wave my hand in her face. She doesn't even blink. "Angela?"

Nothing.

Oh my God. I can't breathe. I can't even see, now, because the tears are falling freely and blurring my vision. I can't wipe them away because my hands are crusted with dirt and blood.

I just stand there, moving from one to the other, hoping that one of them will say, *Oh, hey, there you are!* But Justin has his phone up to his ear and is staring at the ceiling. I can hear the phone ringing, and then a familiar voice says "Yep?" on the other end. There's only one person I know who answers the phone like that.

"Mr. Levesque?" Justin says into the receiver.

My breath hitches. *Dad.*

The tears fall harder. If he were here, everything would be better. My heart twists with the thought of everything I'd done to get away from him. I was so, so stupid. How could I have wanted that? How could I have thought that would be better? I want him here. I want him to wrap his arms around me and tell me he loves me, that I'm his girl. Never in my life have I wanted that so much. I reach for the phone, crying, "Give that to me!" But even though Justin doesn't move, just stands there with one hand holding the phone and the other hand pinching his other ear closed, I can't touch him. Something is wrong. I touch, and yet I feel nothing. I reach for where the phone is, but my hands pass through it like it's made of air. I cannot snatch it from him.

Justin says, "There's a problem with Ki. She's missing."

I'm sobbing now. "No, I'm not. Justin. I'm *right here.*"

But it's useless. I drop my head, letting the tears puddle on the floor, with my blood. So, so much blood. Don't they notice that? Don't they notice anything about me?

Justin looks at the ceiling and exhales deeply. "It's my

fault," he says to my father. "I was the one who convinced her to come up here."

I can hear my father's voice on the other end, an octave higher with worry. Though I can't make out the words, I know what he says: "I'll be right up. I'm coming. I'm leaving right now."

Oh, Dad, I think, as I stare at the growing puddle of blood at my feet, *I'm so sorry. But it's too late.*

CHAPTER NINETEEN

I don't know how much later, I find myself wandering the woods in the blackness. It's dark, and yet I can see. I'm not cold or hot, I'm not anything. My feet don't make a sound, and though there are brambles and roots popping out of the earth, my footing is sure, as if I'm walking a well-known path, and nothing touches me. My wound seeps blood endlessly, but it doesn't hurt.

I don't know how this happened. One moment I was talking to Jack, and . . . Oh, no, I was thinking of kissing him. I wanted to, so badly. Somehow, though I can't feel anything else, I can still feel my face aflame with embarrassment.

Did *Jack* do this to me?

I think of his last words. *If you want to help us, you need to go across. Now.*

But going across would mean . . . No, it's not possible.

Dead. Am I dead? And now, obviously, I don't want to go across. I can't. And yet I don't remember telling him that; I was too busy wishing for other things. But he was a vision.

Only a vision, *my* vision. How could something made of air kill a living being? Could he take a knife, the same knife he'd used to slash at Trey, and plunge it into my stomach? Of course, to other people, he may have been air, but to me, he was more than real. I can still taste his vile lips and feel the muscles of his body straining under his shirt. Maybe being real to me was all it took for him to have the power to claim my life.

Trey warned me to stay away from Jack. What did he say? *You love your life? You love your daddy? You want to get back home to him?*

Oh God, yes. Yes, I'd give anything.

Trey. I snap back to the moment when he reached down and touched my ankle. The calming effect it had on me, the cozy, comfortable sensation that spread over my body as he massaged out all the pain, all the wrong, with his fingertip. And suddenly I am running. I stop clutching my stomach and dart among the trees, calling to him. "Trey!" My voice sounds different as it echoes among the tall pines, so that for a moment I'm not convinced it's mine. It's frantic, yes, but also deeper, more mature. And I don't know where I'm going, and yet I know the path well. I know this place like a newborn baby knows its mother.

Trey is ahead of me on the path. His eyes are downcast, his hands in his pockets so that the blood from his wound is a crimson racing stripe on the side of his dirty jeans. He sighs as I approach. "I've failed, haven't I?"

I reach down and lift up my shirt, exposing my belly. The

few places that are not stained the color of rust are a sick, marbled white. The wound itself is an ugly slit right beside my navel, bubbling thickly with black, like an oil spill. I whisper, desperate, "You can help me. You can heal it, right?"

"Aw, Kiandra." He looks into my eyes, and I know the answer immediately. But that won't do. That is not enough. He's done miracles before and called them child's play. There has to be something he can do.

"No. Don't tell me that. You can do something! You have to!"

He reaches for my hand. Before, his body was so cold, and now his fingers are warm when they brush on my wrist. I want him to use them as he did before, to heal, so I take them in my bloody hand and guide them to my stomach. He lets me pull them only so far before he gently takes them away and shakes his head. "Kiandra. It won't work."

"But it has to. It *has* to," I whimper. "I can't be . . ." But I can't say the word. My lips have forbidden its passage. "I'm only seventeen. I'm going to graduate this month. I'm going to USM. I got in, early acceptance . . ." I think of my dad, taking me out to Friendly's for an ice cream sundae when I told him the news. He'd been beaming. The thought wracks my body with a torrent of sobs. "It's not over for me. *Please.*"

He doesn't say a word, but his face is somber, his eyes are glassy. Is he crying, too? And then I move beside him and see a ghastly sight, just off the path. A body, lying supine among the dead pine needles. A familiar powder-blue jacket, now ripped open, white batting spilling out. A spray of blond hair, greenish in the moonlight and marred with bits of dead leaves and dirt. Eyes open, unblinking. *My* eyes. They'd stared back at me in the mirror every day of my life, and now they're just glistening marbles, staring forever at the sky, at God. And then I see the blood. So much blood, everywhere.

I bring my hands to my mouth, thinking my breath will warm them, but there is no breath in me. My body is shaking and my knees weaken, like two branches ready to snap. Trey pulls me toward him, and it's then I notice we're on a small outcropping, directly over the river. He holds me in his arms, and the moonlight dancing on the ripples is just a sad reminder that things are changing, and will always change, whether I'm ready for them or not.

By morning, my tears have dried, leaving two tight, salty tracks on my cheeks. I sit up, hoping that I'm with Justin, that everything in the past day was just a horrible nightmare. But I'm on the riverbank, and the new sunlight is dappling the water, making its surface so bright that I have this inexplicable urge to jump in, to feel the waves washing over me. Strangely, the river is no longer menacing to me, and I no longer shiver when I look at it. I glance around, blinking. In the morning light, everything has a new, sharper edge to it, with the colors more vivid, the angles more defined. It's as if in life I had a veil over my eyes, and suddenly I'm seeing everything clearly for the first time.

I rub my eyes and pull my jacket up over my belly. The wound looks fresh. It begins to bleed anew, flooding over the waistband of my jeans. I slide my jacket back into place and the tears begin to fall again.

I've almost forgotten about Trey. When I turn around, I'm embarrassed to see that I must have fallen asleep in his arms and used his chest as a pillow, because there's a spot of drool on his shirt. And here I thought dead people didn't have to worry about things like that. He doesn't notice, though. He's wide awake and staring at me. "Feeling better?" he asks, his voice gentle.

His wound, the knife slash on his forearm, isn't bleeding. I point to mine. "Will this ever stop?"

He nods. "When you're not thinking on it. Let it alone."

"Are you kidding?" How am I supposed to forget about this massive, ugly thing in my middle? The blood is running down my thighs. My intestines could slip out at any moment.

When I look up, his wound has opened, and blood begins to bubble on the surface. He shakes his head. "I know. Easier said than done."

I shiver in the morning air; my teeth are chattering in a steady drumbeat. I'm not cold; my hands are their normal color, not the deathly blue that they sometimes turn in freezing temperatures. Funny that my hands look more alive now. I think of the last sight I witnessed before Trey pulled me to him and I fell asleep in his arms. It was my body, lying off the path. Dead. I don't want to see it. Don't want to at all, yet still I find myself craning my neck, searching it out. Maybe if I don't see it, this will all prove to be a horrible nightmare and I'll be able to go home.

Trey puts a hand on my shoulder. "I moved it. Down near the river. Didn't think you'd want to see it again."

I sigh, grateful and sad all at once. "I should have listened to you. You knew he was going to try to hurt me. I just didn't think . . ." I swipe uselessly at the tears. "Why? Because he hates my mother?"

He's slowly stroking his thumb back and forth over my collarbone. "Don't worry yourself over the whys. It's done."

Then I say, "Jack told me he killed you. Is that true?"

He looks surprised for a moment. "Wow. Guess lying never got him nowhere, so now he's trying out telling the truth. Yeah. It's true."

"He's a monster. First you, now me." I shake my head. "He killed you because you turned him in, right? He'd killed someone else? A little girl?"

His face hardens. "Him? Nah. I don't like talking about it. Happened a long time ago, so it don't matter anyway. Let's see." Staring at my wound, he unbuttons and removes his shirt. His arms and chest are tan and muscled. I find myself blushing and looking away as he comes close to me and gently presses the shirt against my stomach. It doesn't hurt, not at all. His hair flops in his face and when he leans down I can smell it. It's like leaves and fresh wind and woods. And then I see that his shirt is sopping with my blood, and remember last night.

That horrible, horrible night. I don't even hate Justin or Ange anymore; I don't think I ever did. I just miss them. I miss those dull, sloppy kisses Justin used to give me. I miss shopping with Ange. The only thing I ever wore bikinis for was sunbathing at the back of the house, but the last time we went out, I'd found a cute pink one. My first thought when I look at that wound is *I guess bikinis are out.* Then my mind travels over everything else that's out, too. Kissing. Shopping. Sunbathing. Talking to Ange. Everything. I fold up into a ball and start to cry again.

I feel Trey's arm around me. "Hey, hey, hey. Kiandra. It's not all bad."

"What's good about it?" I sniff.

He straightens. "Well, for one, you get to spend time with me. That's pretty . . . well, I'll just go and say it. Great." He smiles broadly.

My jaw just hangs open. It's the first time he's ever joked. Aren't the dead supposed to be more . . . sullen? Hopeless?

"What?" he says, noticing my surprise. "You think dead people can't have fun?"

It never did cross my mind. It doesn't seem like they have an awful lot to celebrate. "Well, yeah. You've always been so—"

"Before, I was worried about saving your sorry backside. Don't have to worry about that no more." He shakes his head at me, and when I start to apologize, he says, "No point in fretting over it now. I'll catch hell later." I'm just starting to feel bad again when he says, "And you still got those powers of yours. You want to try them out?"

"Powers?" I study my hands. "Like what?"

He stands up. "Like a lot of things. Here." He reaches down and molds a few wet black leaves together into a small mound. "Go 'head."

I stare at him. "What do you want me to do?"

"Light it on fire."

I let out a short laugh. "I can't—" But before the words come out, sparks fly from the center of it and a fire consumes it, leaping into the air. I can't even breathe. "I didn't do that. Tell me I didn't do that."

He shrugs. "You didn't do that." Then he grins. "Okay, yeah, you did."

I shake my head. "You're not telling me that all I need to do is think of something and it will happen?" I ask, horrified. Because how often have I thought strange things, like wishing that it would be ninety degrees during the long Maine winter, or wanting the Academy Awards to be broadcast from my high school gymnasium?

"It's a little more than that. You've got to want it." He looks at the fire. "You got some power, girl. I wasn't able to light fire for a couple of weeks, at least."

"Really?"

"Yeah. And that's a small thing. Just you wait. I'll learn you. It'll be fun."

"Okay," I say. Maybe it will be. It won't be life, but it might be interesting.

He smiles. "So, you ready?"

"For what?"

"Don't tell me you don't already know the third good thing about being here?" he asks, raising his eyebrows. "I'll take you across now."

I gasp. "What? Now? You mean . . ."

"Sure. You want to see your momma, don't you?" He studies me, then asks, "What's got you in a tizzy?"

"I'm fine," I say, but even as I do my teeth clack together. He tilts his head to one side and his expression says, *Level with me*. "It's—it's just that I'm cold."

I know he's the type to remove his shirt and give it to me to keep me warm, but he's already given me his shirt, for the wound. I expect that he'll wrap an arm around me, but he doesn't. He lowers his head and says, "Quit playing. The dead don't feel warm or cold."

"Oh," I mutter. But they can obviously feel other things. Fear. Indecision. Regret. Hate. "I just . . . My mom left me when I was seven. She just left. For ten years, I've been without her. And I've . . . I've come to . . ." The words "hate her" are on my lips, but they won't come out. "I just don't understand why."

He stands there, nodding as if I make perfect sense, which makes me feel a little better.

"Her powers are dying? Is she . . . sick?" I ask.

He crosses his arms in front of him. "Who told you that? Let me guess. No, she's just as strong as she has ever been. Once again, you go and do something I tell you not to. I told you not to listen to him." He looks down the path, toward the river. "Look, I been kind of lax in my duties. I got to be going."

He starts walking down the narrow path toward the Outfitters. I tremble as he leaves. I don't want to see Jack again. But at the same time, I do. Definitely, I can still feel indecision and fear. "Where are you going?"

He turns and smiles, and like he's reading my mind, says, "There ain't nothing more Jack wants to do to you now."

"Oh." But that isn't enough. I'm ashamed of how I acted around him. My behavior with Jack is inexplicable. The force pulling me to him was so strong, and I'm so afraid that even after the horrible things he's done to me, I'll still somehow be drawn to him. But I can't tell Trey that. It doesn't make any sense, even to me.

"You can still come with me," he says.

I stand, brush the pine needles from my backside, and follow him. As I walk, I marvel at how I can almost see every individual grain of dirt on the ground, at how I can almost hear every insect marching along its path. Now that the sun has risen, everything takes on a warm orange hue, and the entire sky is a shade of lavender I've seen only in small streaks during the most colorful of sunsets. The river, once black, now looks clear and inviting, like the Caribbean Sea. "Everything looks so . . . alive," I whisper. *I guess compared to me, anything is.*

He turns back. "You're different. So you see things different."

"I feel strange. I used to be so afraid of the river. Now I want to . . . I don't know. Dive in."

He grabs a stick and starts swishing it through the brush

as we walk. "Told you. You're different. In death, you become what you most wanted to be in life."

I wrinkle my nose. "Like what?"

He shrugs. "You figure it out. Don't you know what you wanted to be?"

I think. Shake my head. Before I know it, we're at the pier near the Outfitters. There's a different boat there, one I've never seen. It's just a primitive raft, kind of like something out of *Tom Sawyer*. A line of people, waiting patiently, stretches up the hill. It's a motley crew, some young, some old. They're not dressed in wet suits. One man is wearing a Speedo. A little girl is standing there, naked, sucking her thumb and crying quietly. The strangest thing is how eerily silent everything is, though there are so many people there. Most of them look a little dazed. Trey runs his hands through his hair and whistles. "Sheesh," he mutters. "I'm gonna catch hell, that's for sure."

"What—" I begin, but I know. I know who these people are.

Trey walks to the front of the line and cups his hands around his mouth. "Proceed in an orderly fashion," he calls.

The line moves. Most people put their heads down and walk, ever so slowly, onto the raft. I swallow as I look at the little girl. I don't care if these people cannot feel cold. I pull off my jacket and hurry to wrap it around her. I notice that it's no longer sopping with blood, which is good, but the second I notice that, I can feel the wound open up in my stomach with a sickening pop, like a hungry mouth. The little girl is so tiny and thin. When I stand next to her, she eagerly takes my hand and presses herself against my leg.

The raft fills with people. We all press together. The girl looks up to me gratefully, her dark blue eyes rimmed with tears. I didn't mean to go across yet, but I can't leave her. I hear Trey's voice telling people, "Step to the back of the raft. Room enough for everyone. That's right. No pushing." People crowd against us and we're forced to the very end of the raft, and by the time I turn around, I can no longer see him.

A confused man, maybe in his twenties, is standing next to me. He's wearing swim trunks. He smells like alcohol and keeps wiping blood away from his eye because there's a wound so big, it looks like half of his head has caved in. I wonder if he knows it. I shield the little girl's eyes from the sight of him when he says, "Where am I? Where are we going?" But nobody answers. Everyone else, like me, seems to know already. Drops of blood slip from his chin, turning pink when they hit the clear water. Even that is beautiful.

We set off. I expect the river to carry us downstream, as it did when Hugo tried to take me across in the kayak. But it's like we're crossing a calm, glassy lake. The boat does not pitch and toss. We simply glide, as if we're skating across a frozen pond. There is a slight breeze, and from the middle of the river, I see that the sun is bright over the tall pines. This is not what I expected at all. When I look back to the east bank, I notice that the line that looked a hundred people long is now gone. Somehow, we all fit on this small raft. At first I think that's impossible, but in a world where nothing is as I expected, maybe it is possible. Maybe many things that are impossible in life are possible here.

The raft comes to a slow, easy stop at the west bank, and people begin to disembark. I wait patiently with the little girl, who is now smiling at me shyly. "Are you an angel?" she asks.

"No," I say, smiling at her.

She says, "Mommy told me the angels would meet me when she put me under the water."

I put my hand to my mouth to hide my shock. Instantly the tears start to come. I miss my dad and my friends so much. I miss my bedroom. I will never see it again. I will never see any of them again.

"I want to go home," the girl whispers, and I hug her close, because I do, too. This new world is at once beautiful and terrifying.

When the rest of the people have left the raft, I see them climbing up a path through the forest in a single, orderly line. Trey is standing at the pier. At first he's happy to see me. "Hey, thought you were staying behind," he says, but then he sees that I've been crying. My face is probably all red, like it usually gets when I cry. Or maybe it isn't. Maybe being dead makes that different, too. He doesn't bother to ask me what's wrong. I guess it's pretty obvious.

I squint to see across the river. I can just make out a few people, dressed in black wet suits, setting up over there for the new day's rafting trip. Jealousy tightens my chest. I never thought I'd be jealous of people going rafting, but right now, I'd give anything to be one of them. I'd give anything to be at the beginning of this weekend. Or even better, at the beginning of this week. I'd tell Justin I had a change of heart and now I really wanted to go to prom, and he'd take me, because that's the kind of guy he is. And Angela would understand, because that's the kind of girl she is. They love me. When I think about how wonderful they are, how alike they are, more tears fall, so many I know it would be useless to wipe them away with the back of my hand.

Trey leans down and starts to play got-your-nose with the little girl. She giggles. I think of my mom. "My mom used to play that with me," I say.

He nods. "Learned it from her. Good way to get the young ones to calm down."

And calm the little girl is. She's clinging to him now. He must like my mother. Respect her. Why else would he talk about her, learn things from her? I'm not sure if that makes me like him more, or less.

The little girl climbs up on his back, wrapping her pudgy fingers around his neck. I whisper, "Her mom murdered her."

His face is somber, but he nods like it's nothing unexpected. I guess he's heard a lot of horror stories in his job. He looks at his palms quickly, then wipes them on his jeans, but not before I see that the scabs there have opened. He leaves ruddy marks on his thighs, but his jeans are dirty anyway, so it's hardly noticeable. He catches me watching and says, "All in a day's work."

"I thought you said my mother was supposed to lead people across."

"Normally she would, but she's conserving her powers. She needs them all. 'Cause of what I told you."

"And you don't have . . . powers that can do it for you?"

"Nah. The Mistress of the Waters might, but not me. I'm just a son of an oilman from Tulsa, Oklahoma. Ain't royalty or nothing, like you."

I snort. "I'm not royalty. My dad clips coupons." He doesn't say anything, so I say, "Tulsa? Is that where you're from?"

"Moved out there when I was six. Born in New York. My daddy was a big-time executive at the Buick Motor Company. You ever hear of them?" I nod. "Well, when I was six he moved us out to Tulsa to start his oil business, and it did pretty well. Guess he was a millionaire. Can you imagine that? Me, a millionaire? We had *two* cars, believe it or not. We was wealthy. I was on my way to Harvard that fall."

I stare at him. "Harvard?"

He nods. "It's a university in Boston. You know it? It's still there?"

"Um, yeah. I just didn't . . . I mean . . ." I blush because there's no tactful way to say what I'm thinking, that he was uneducated and poor. "So, what happened?"

He looks at me like I have three heads. "I died was what. My dad lost everything in the crash. House was too crowded, so after I graduated I got out and hopped myself a train up north. Ended up on the Bel Del, working odd jobs so I could get up to college. That's where I met up with Jack."

He bows his head, almost shameful. "You know how that all turned out."

"I'm sorry."

"Hey, it's probably a good thing I didn't go to Harvard. I'd probably end up living in a house like them friends of yours. One that makes your meals for you and wipes your mouth with a napkin afterward." He points across the river and laughs. Then he puts his chin to his chest. "Do worry about my momma, though. My body was never found. Not that they looked much."

"But you said you became a legend in twelve counties. About the boy who couldn't swim?"

"Where I died, yeah. Not where my momma lived. There were a couple of witnesses, but none of them helped me. All too afraid. They all came up with the rhyme to protect Jack, make it look like an accident. My momma's the worrying kind. Probably spent her whole life wondering what happened to me. I wrote her letters sometimes, when I was alive. But I never saw her again."

I think about my father. The thought sends a stab of pain through my chest. I'm never going to see him again.

The little girl on his back has fallen asleep, and she looks like an angel herself with her eyelids fluttering and her cheeks rosy. I look around as we walk past the cemetery I'd spotted a day ago. It's an old one. Most of the headstones are crumbling and faded, but I can make out some of the years. Most are from the 1700s. The green of the trees frames all the gray stone, making the place look more romantic than frightening. Trey pays no attention to it, just follows this worn stone staircase up a hill, into a line of trees. "Where are we going?"

He stops. "That's right. You didn't want to see your momma yet. She's up at the top of the hill. She likes to greet newcomers. You want to wait here while I bring her up?" He motions toward the little girl.

I look up the pathway, which ends in pine trees the color of new grass, and at the lavender sky. "Does she know about me?"

He nods.

I bite my lip. "She doesn't want to see me. She was trying to push me away."

"No, she was trying to *protect* you, kid. She'll want to see you. Trust me. Mommas worry."

He's staring at me with eyes so intensely blue, almost the exact color the river is now, I wonder if that's me perceiving things differently or if that's the way they've always been. Before, they'd been so dark, troubled. I look down and realize he has his hand out for me to take. I wrap my fingers around his, expecting to feel the sores I'd seen before, but, strangely, his fingers are soft, maybe even softer than mine.

When we begin to walk again, he mutters under his breath, "You, she'll want to see. Me, she'll want to *kill.* Guess I'm in luck it's too late for that."

"I'm sorry," I say again. "I'll tell her it's my fault. You did everything you could. I'm just a stubborn pain in the ass."

"You said it," he mutters, turning away, but even though his head is down and his hair is in his face, I see the hint of a smile.

"Hey! I think I liked you better when you were all doom and gloom," I say, punching his arm.

"'Cause I was easier to ignore?" he asks, and by then we've reached the landing at the top of the hill. Though we've climbed pretty far, I'm not out of breath. Maybe because I don't need to breathe? I try holding my breath to see, but my cheeks bulge like a chipmunk's, right when Trey turns around to look at me. He laughs. "Are you holding your breath?"

"Um, I—"

"Don't bother. Every dead person's tried it out one time or another. But even ghosts need air."

I feel myself blushing. "But what will happen to me if I don't breathe? I can't die."

"Nah, but you'll lose your shine."

"Shine?"

"We all have a light when we come here. We call it our shine. See yours?" He points to my hand. With his bluish, dead fingers next to mine, the difference is striking. My skin is glowing white, not unlike the surface of the moon. His is more bluish. Some of the people who were milling about when we arrived looked almost watery, blurry. Blinking did no good. Their bodies were tinged with dark blue. Even in sun, they were in shadow. "When you pass on, you don't lose your life all at once. Sure, you lose your body, but your life is still there. Shine's your human life. The longer you're here, in our world, the more shine you lose. The more you fade, the more your powers fade."

I study Trey. Compared to the new souls who've just traversed the river, he is faded, bluish.

"Other things affect your shine. Your body being laid to rest is one of them. And, of course, you got to want to move on," he says. "Some people keep their shine."

In answer to my questioning look, he says, "Some people don't want to go. Either they want to be alive or they want something else they could only get in life, and it eats away at them. They become evil spirits. Fiends."

"Fiends?" I murmur, thinking of Jack, of how brightly he shone, how intensely hard it was to even look at him. But Trey had shone brightly, too. "What do they do that's so evil?"

He opens his mouth to speak, but stops when he reaches the top of the hill. I come up behind him, and I can see stone walls, crumbling as much as the headstones on the riverbank. It's a small house, or what remains of it. There is no roof, but the branches of old trees with fresh new leaves hang over it like a canopy. Ivy crawls up the black stones, almost completely claiming them. Here, the only sound is the twittering of birds. The line of people winds up ahead, but it's perfectly silent; every one of them looks around, awestruck. It's so peaceful and lush and green. I think I could fall asleep on this carpet of soft spring grass and never wake up.

I forget what we're talking about when I see her. She is

a small woman, as unremarkable in appearance now as she was in life. And yet I can't take my eyes off her. The world slows and silences. She smiles and welcomes each person with a hug. Her hair and face are fair, and despite the limited sunlight leaking through the leaves above, something about her glitters like gold. She moves like a leaf on the wind, so gracefully, and those she smiles at seem to be affected by her, as immediately they begin to smile, too. She's wearing an ordinary white baseball shirt with red sleeves, with a giant P on it, for the Phillies. I know it because she'd worn it all the time. She'd gotten it at my first—and last—baseball game at Veterans Stadium in Philadelphia. Somehow I'd expected her to be wearing a long, regal robe, or a crown, or something. But no, it's just her, just my mom, looking exactly the same. The same as the day she died.

Suddenly I'm back in my bedroom, lying flat on my back in bed, with the summer heat pressing down on me and the iridescent ripples on the walls. My parents were weirdly absent from my life that summer, talking in hushed whispers about "adult things" they said I didn't need to know about, so Lannie became my best and only friend. One day I'd been playing with Lannie all afternoon, and Lannie had been playing her usual games, pretending to be hanging by the neck from trees, making herself invisible when we played hide-and-seek. It put me in a foul mood, and I just wanted to get away from her. So I was alone in my bedroom with a pillow over my head to keep the visions away when my mother walked in. My mother tried to take the pillow off my head but I yelled at her. She told me she had something to say, something important, but I screamed at her to leave me alone.

I thought she'd fight it, tell me to behave or something, but she just did as I told her to. She put her cold, clammy hand on my bare knee and whispered an "I love you," then walked out of my room. There wasn't anything different about that, she was constantly saying she loved me, so much that I forgot what it meant. A minute later I heard the screen door slam and feet swishing on the grass. I scrambled to look out my window. In that red-and-white baseball shirt, she was walking toward the river. The way she moved should have made me nervous; she walked very deliberately, not like she was just going for a stroll. And she wouldn't ever leave me alone in the house, not even for a minute, to go get the mail. But I was so angry, partly at Lannie and partly at myself for not having made any real friends, that I turned away and shoved the pillow over my head and held it there until the sirens screamed me back into reality.

I ran downstairs. I can still remember the look on my father's face when he came home from work and the police told him that several people had seen his wife walk into the river. Some had dove in to rescue her, but she'd never been found. His body kind of crumpled and he grabbed my shoulder so tight that pain rocketed down my arm. "I didn't think she'd go so soon," he sobbed. I'd found those words strange at first, but the more I thought about it, the more I knew what he meant. Maybe it was how sad my mother always seemed. She always smiled at me, but it was as if she worked to achieve that smile. Whenever she thought she was alone, I'd catch her frowning, her brow furrowed as if the weight of everything was on her shoulders. Deep down, I guess we both always knew she'd leave us.

I'm so engrossed in the memory, I don't see anything else around me, only her form, coming nearer. When she is close to me, she puts a hand on my cheek. Her hand is cold and clammy, as I remember it. "Kiandra," she says. "How I've missed you." She pulls me into a hug. Her smell is the same, sweet and clean.

There are so many questions I want to ask, but for now I just allow her arms to swallow me up and I press my cheek against her shoulder so hard that it hurts. "Mom," I say. It comes out hoarse and watery, and I realize I'm crying.

It's only then I see Trey standing beside me, fidgeting nervously. When I pull back, my mother's giving him a look I often had directed at me whenever I did something wrong. Quickly I say, "It's not Trey's fault. He wanted me to leave but I'm too stubborn."

She contemplates this for a moment. "That is true," she says with a hint of a smile.

I frown. I don't like her professing to know me. She *left* me. When I was seven, I wanted her so much, *ached* for her. The pain from those days was so bad, I can still feel it, but it's an old wound. It's been a long time since I've wanted her. Now, standing in front of her, hugging her, it's like being presented to someone only slightly more familiar than a stranger. All

I know is that I don't want those wounds to be reopened. I don't want to get so close that I ache and ache and nothing can fill that hole.

Trey speaks up. "I thought I'd show her around."

I'm relieved by the suggestion, but my mother shakes her head. "I need to talk to my daughter in private."

The thought makes my stomach tighten. Trey is already turning back down the path when my mother tells him to wait a moment. She takes him aside and says, "I have a job for you. On the east side," then whispers something into his ear. He listens intently, gives me a nervous glance, and then heads out. I'm amazed. Here, she is a leader. At home, I was the only person she was in charge of, and she was gentle, quiet, even when I misbehaved. She certainly never ordered me around. It just seems so unlike her. I refuse to be impressed. Before I can stop my gaping, she turns her eyes toward my face. She motions for me to follow her, but it's like my feet have rooted in the ground. I don't want to go. I need to get away. Just be alone. To sort out this whirlwind of emotions inside me. She gives me a look as if to say *What are you waiting for?*

But I can't. I can't bring myself to move. This is my mother. The mother I lost so many years ago. *Standing in front of me.* "I, um, have to use the bathroom," I manage.

Her face breaks into a small smile before melting into a frown. She shakes her head. "Kiandra . . ."

I can tell by her expression that I've flubbed, that obviously dead people don't need to do such things. Heat rises in my face. I peel my feet from the ground and trail behind her into the woods. As we walk she says, "How is your father?" as if he's some acquaintance and not the man she was married to for ten years.

"Fine," I say, forcing the word out of my throat.

"I miss him," she says softly. Then she stops and looks at me. "I missed you. You've grown up so well. You're beautiful."

"And you missed it all," I mutter.

She nods. "I know. I feel bad about that. But obviously your father didn't do such a bad—"

"No. He didn't. You're right." I don't mean to snap, but my words come out that way. Once again I feel like I'm seven years old, back in that house on the river, having a tantrum.

She stares at me. "You're angry."

With her eyes boring into me, I get a familiar feeling. I feel the waterworks starting. I'm going to cry again. Whenever she would look at me that way, for breaking a vase in the living room, for hiding my new dress when I ripped it, or whatever, I would always stare into those eyes and cave. I'd run into her arms and beg her for forgiveness, beg her to love me again. But not now. Now I'm beyond that. I don't need her approval anymore. And I'm not going to cry for her. "Wouldn't *you* be?"

She sucks in her bottom lip. "Your father didn't tell you anything."

"No," I say, looking away and hardening myself. "And after a while I stopped asking. I know why he wouldn't. Suicide isn't something you discuss with a seven-year-old."

"I'll never forgive myself for not saying goodbye to you properly. It was just . . . too hard. I wanted to. But I knew if you cried and begged me to stay, I wouldn't be able to go through with it. And I needed to." She stares hard at me. "I *needed* to. For you."

I squint at her. "For me? That's stupid."

"I know it might have been cruel to leave. But it would have been even crueler if I'd stayed." She sighs. "I had a brain stem glioma. Do you know what that is?"

Now we're alone among the tall pines. The wind rustles through them but makes no sound, so I swear I can hear my heart beating. "Brain stem? You mean . . ."

"A tumor. In my brain. A very serious one. The prognosis was bad, and some days the pain was unbearable. I talked it over with your father. If I was going to die, I wanted to have some control over it. So that was what I planned. I meant to say goodbye. Really, I did."

I swallow. "Why didn't Dad tell me?"

"Did you ask him?"

"I didn't think I had to! I thought I knew what happened. I thought you . . ." I know I didn't think anything at the time. I thought my mom had gone away, and my father wouldn't say more than that. Over time, though, I put the pieces together, and it formed a picture that could mean only one thing. Suicide. And it *was* suicide. She didn't *have* to do it. She could have had more time with me, and she chose something else. Even a day more, an hour, a minute—all that precious time we could have had together was thrown away. I stand there on the path, shaking. "You should have stayed with us."

"And have you see me so weak? So sick? I wasn't your mother anymore. I couldn't care for you. I was helpless."

"I wouldn't have cared! I just wanted you. Sick or healthy. I didn't care!" I shout.

"You wouldn't have had me either way. The doctors gave me three months to live. I was beyond chemotherapy. It was too late."

"But even a few more days," I protest, but it comes out soft because suddenly I feel very weak.

"You're tired," she says. "You need rest."

I remember how she used to usher me up to my bedroom every time I acted out of line, saying, "You're tired and need to rest." No, she just wants to be done with me. I bet ghosts don't even need to rest, just like they don't need to use the bathroom. The thought makes me more bitter than ever. "I'm fine. I wish you would have stayed."

She is silent for a moment. "And I wish you had stayed alive. You should have left when Trey told you. But we all can't have what we want, now, can we?" She sounds like she did whenever I told her I wanted dessert, never mean, just sweetly condescending. In my mind's eye, I'm in the kitchen, reaching for a bag of cookies in the pantry. She slams the door and smiles at me. *We all can't have what we want, now, can we?*

I feel a new wash of tears fall over my cheeks. It was futile to think I could harden myself against her. She is my mother. I was deluding myself when I said I didn't care. She is my sun. Even if she hated me, that fact would never change.

"You don't even want me here now. You sent Trey to make sure I stayed away, because you didn't want me with you."

She puts her hands on my shoulders. "Listen to me, Kiandra. I want you. It hurts me terribly not to be with you, but it made me happy to know that you were having a life. More than anything, I wanted you to live. To be happy and *live*." She enunciates the last word as if teaching it to me for the first time. "You were happy there, without me, weren't you?"

I wipe the tears from my cheeks and look out toward the east bank. I think of Justin, and my father. I wonder if Dad has made it up to the river yet. I wonder how I'll look when they find my body. How they'll react. The thought of my father seeing me that way twists my heart. I'm his everything. That's what he said to me, about a thousand times, on that ride up from New Jersey. He kept chewing on the inside of his cheek and looking over at me with crazed eyes. *You're my everything. I won't let anything happen to you.* I nod.

She smiles a little. "You had a boyfriend, didn't you? What is his name?"

I nod again, less forcefully this time. I'm not really sure what we were, as of last night. I guess we were still boyfriend and girlfriend. "Justin," I say, but I'm back to thinking about my dad. *You're my everything.* More tears slide over my cheeks. "But I can't stop thinking about Dad. This will kill him."

"Yes. I know it will." She bows her head for a moment, then moves closer to me, and I think she's going to hug me again. Instead, she leans in close to my ear. I feel the familiar sweep of her lips on my cheek. It sends the world reeling for me, but not as much as her next words. Very quietly, she says, "And that is why I am going to send you back."

It takes a moment to register. I search for another meaning, but can't think of one. "What . . . You don't mean that . . ."

"Oh, Kiandra. It's not that I don't want you."

"No, it's not that. It's . . ." Maybe this is a misunderstanding. She didn't see the wound in my body. She didn't see how much blood I lost. There's no way I could go back to *living*. That's not possible. I've heard of people who die for a few minutes and come back to life, but I've been dead for hours. "What are you talking about?"

"You will have this power, too. Many of our ancestors do. We are the only ones."

I shake my head. "Are you talking about . . . making me alive again?"

She doesn't have to say a word. Her expression speaks volumes.

I stop breathing. "But how? That can't be done."

She crosses her arms. "It can be. But if I do this for you, you must leave here and never come back. Not until you are one hundred years old. Preferably later. And please realize it's not because I don't want to see you again. I will see you again."

"It's impossible," I whisper.

She puts a hand on mine. Her eyes glint with pride. "I assure you, I can do it. As long as certain conditions are met. I would prove it to you now, but I need to ensure a little something before I can start. Trey is working on that. Now I have some duties to attend to. Do not stray too far."

She brushes my wrist with her thumb and turns to walk back to the crumbling stone house. I'm just standing there, numb, in disbelief. The sun is hot on my face, and it's then I realize that we've climbed through the woods, and I'm standing on a peak overlooking the river. The wind blows hard and cold against my skin. Down below, yellow rafts dot the river, returning from the day's white-water expedition. I can see across to the east bank. Trey is there somewhere, performing some task for my mother, in order to send me back. *Send me back.* To the living. How is that possible? If it is, why can't she send herself back? Why didn't she kill me herself to spend just a few more days with me, if she knew she could send me back? I turn to ask her the hundreds of questions percolating in my mind, but she has already disappeared among the trees.

CHAPTER TWENTY

Still not feeling right alone, I head back toward the old stone house. Trey must be back with a new group, because a new long line is snaking up from the dock, all people I don't recognize. It's hard to believe so many people have died on the water. The little girl I saw before is having her hair braided by an old woman. She smiles at me and waves. I'm about to go over there when I catch a bright light shining through the pines. Trey. I move away and see another figure beside him. My mother. He's listening intently, and I can tell from his expression that he's not happy. Something's wrong.

He scowls and storms out into the sunlit path, nearly colliding with me. The worry on his face quickly dissolves into a smile. "Hey!"

I study him. "What was that all about back there?" When he shrugs, I say, "You looked upset. Is something wrong?"

"Nothing for you to be worrying about," he says, digging his hands into the back pockets of his jeans. He looks over each shoulder, for someone, I guess—my mother? "You want me to show you round now?"

"I don't see what the point is. She's sending me back," I whisper. "Did you know she could do that?"

He gives me a small nod, then pulls on my sleeve, beckoning me back up the pathway. He leads me on a new path, which begins to slope downward, toward the river. I follow him silently, thinking about the fiends, about the sad, angry souls that still miss their human lives. Did Jack do this to me because he's jealous of me and the life I have?

Finally, when we're almost near the river, Trey says to me, "Yeah."

"If you knew that, then why is it such a big deal? Why have you been watching me so closely—"

"It *is* a big deal. You don't understand. Your momma has powers none of us have. But it's not an unlimited supply. Bringing someone back has never been done before, and it will weaken her. We don't know how much. It might take away all her power."

"All her shine?"

He looks at the ground. "Yeah."

"And then what?"

"She's gone. Like I said, I don't know where. And that relation of yours? The one I told you about? That person will take over. And I don't expect things will be very good here after that."

"Jack?" I ask.

"Yeah. No. I don't know. It's going to be a mess here. But

your momma's right. You got another chance at life. You need to take it."

"You would take it?"

"In a heartbeat."

"But I could take over. I could be the Mistress. Now."

He squints at me. "You don't know nothing yet. And you want that? You want to leave everything behind?"

I don't even have to think about it now. Of course I don't. But I would, if I were needed. I would . . . I stop when I realize that's just what my mother did. And I hated her for it. I don't want to leave my dad and have him hate me. Right now, I don't want to think about it. So I concentrate on Trey, the edges of his form shining so very brightly. Not as luminous as I am, but for someone who has been here since the Great Depression, he's certainly not lost a lot of his glow.

"Your shine," I say gently. "It's so bright. And you've been here so long. It's almost as bright as Jack's."

He looks down, his face reddening. "Yeah. For a long time I wanted to go back. I was like Jack. Bitter. Angry. I volunteered to be a guide just so I could go over to the other side and see what was going on. See what I been missing. And I missed a lot. But I don't mean to go against your momma. She's a good lady. Treated me like my momma would've. I won't do that to her." He looks up at the sky, shakes his head. "But I come to realize there's no point thinking about going back. It can't happen. Not for me. Come on."

We reach the edge of the river. There's a small rowboat

there, tied to a stump. He motions for me to get in, so I do. "Where are we going?" I ask.

"You'll see." He takes up the rope, pushes the boat out a few feet from shore, and hops in.

As he starts to row, I'm suddenly aware what this means. We're going across. To where Justin is. To where my father is. They won't be able to see me. I'm remembering how I was screaming at Justin and Angela, and how they just looked through me. The thought of that empty look in their eyes makes my chest hurt. I don't know if I could stand it if my dad looked through me the same way. "I thought my mom was going to make me alive again?" I ask. "She said that it has to be done quickly."

"Problem with that." He looks over his shoulder. "We need your body. That's what she sent me over to get."

I nearly choke. "My . . . body? Why?"

"Well, it won't do no good if your momma brings you to life and then a month later a fisherman stumbles on your bones, will it?"

"Okay, okay." I shudder at the idea of seeing my lifeless body again. "Did you get it?"

He shakes his head. "It's gone. Someone took it."

"What? Who would do something like that?"

"Don't know. Humans may have found it. Maybe I didn't hide it good enough. That would be a problem." He looks up at the sky, where the sun is beginning to slump from its highest point. "And if we don't have it back before a search party finds it . . . Yeah. It will be too late."

* * *

I slosh in my hiking boots through what feels like thick mud. When I come up on shore and attempt to clean my boots, I realize they're almost perfect. Trey glances at me, and I wonder how the rest of me looks. It feels like I haven't had a shower in ages. I think of my mother, day after day, wearing the same Phillies shirt she died in years ago. I guess I don't need to shower, and that thought makes me instantly miss the heavenly spray of hot water on my face and back. And then I look at Trey and realize I'm being stupid, that unlike him, at least I *have* a chance of getting back, which I'll probably blow if I keep thinking silly things like how much I miss showers.

"I don't understand. What would that person do, if the person took over my mother's rule?"

He says, "A bad ruler here would keep the people angry and bitter, and it's the angry and bitter people who take a long time to come to peace. They stay here."

"Like you."

"Yeah. Like me. Look how long it's taken me to come around. The bigger the kingdom, the more power the ruler has."

"So wait—what you're saying is that if my mom brings me to life again, she will weaken to the point where this person can take over? I will destroy the entire kingdom?"

"Listen. Your momma's gonna take care of you. Don't give up this chance. I wouldn't." He steps onto a boulder and reaches for my hand, but I'm just standing there, not able to move.

"You wouldn't?" I mumble. "Really? I feel like a stupid brat. I got myself into this. I should just accept the consequences."

"Kiandra, I'll be the first to tell you when you are being a brat. You ain't a brat for accepting this."

"No, listen. Jack did this to me. He knew that my mother would try and bring me back. He wants her to do this. He wants to weaken her. If I let her do this, we're just playing into his hands."

He nods, unsurprised, and starts to speak, but I put my hand up to silence him. Because, right then, I realize something. "You knew that all this time, didn't you? Ever since I got here. That's why you've been protecting me. You knew he'd try to hurt me. Why didn't you just tell me?"

"I told you he was dangerous. What more did you want?" He'd been reaching for my hand, but now he just digs both hands into the pockets of his jeans. "You were just a girl who stepped on a hornet's nest, is all. I thought all I needed to do was get you away from the nest. I didn't want you to know about your momma, about this Mistress of the Waters stuff, because I knew you wouldn't leave. I'm sorry, Kiandra, but the only way you're gonna make your momma happy is if you do this. And I'm gonna help her."

"Maybe I don't care about making her happy. Why do you follow her so blindly?" I say, my voice rising an octave. "What has she done for you that you keep bending over backward for her?"

He doesn't say anything, just stands there on top of the

boulder, rocking on his heels. From his expression, I can't even be sure he's listening.

"She's not *your* mother. You may feel guilty about leaving your mother, and your mother may be a saint, but that lady across the river is not her," I say. "My mother was dying and couldn't even say goodbye to me. She might have been sick, but she could have had more time with me, and instead, she left. Why should I care about whether or not I make her happy? And you keep following her around, doing whatever she tells you to. You sound pathetic."

His eyes snap to mine. So he was listening. I catch my breath when I realize all the hurtful things I've just said. His face begins to cloud, from clear indifference to a perfect mix of anger and disappointment. His brow sinks, and lines form around his eyes. Still, he says nothing. I open my mouth to apologize but only a muffled sound comes out, because I don't know what to say. I know what I should do, though. To save him, my mother, the kingdom, I have to leave. I have to run away and never be found.

I turn and run. Trey calls to me to stop, but I keep going. I expect Trey to catch up to me, to grab me, but I am ahead of him, out of his reach. How is it I am so nimble, so graceful? I'm running so fast that everything is a blur around me. The farther I race, the more I know that this is the right thing to do. To be alone, not responsible for anyone else. All at once I feel brave and invincible and athletic, things that I never felt before. The feeling is strangely exhilarating.

I come to a stop when I see something moving among the trees. Slowly, it drags itself along, scraping up the forest floor. Letting the air fill my lungs, I turn. Trey is gone. At first I think it's an awkward, large animal, like a moose, but it stills at the same time I do. I get the feeling it's watching me. Now, through the leaves, I can make out crisp pink cloth. I duck my head lower and see the shoes. Girls' white T-buckle shoes, the surface more scuffs than patent leather. One delicate knee-high is up, and one is pooling around her ankle. I strain to remember her name. "Vi?" My voice is a loud whisper.

I know she can't answer me. Every time she opens her mouth, that foul black mud will pour over her chin. She doesn't come toward me, though. She stays there, perfectly still. The forest is so quiet that I can hear her breathing.

"I know it's you," I call pleasantly, because she's a child, and a jumpy one, and I half expect her to run away. I think I've lost her when she takes one step in the direction she'd been headed, toward the Outfitters, but suddenly she stops. "Stop hiding," I say. "Come on out."

She doesn't move. I wait a minute, but nothing changes. Either the leaves are shuddering in the breeze, or she is.

I step forward, hands out. "I'm not going to hurt you."

When I've moved closer, I can see her eyes, wide and brown as the mud crusting her lips. There's always fear there, but now it's magnified. She's shaking. I peer through the branches and see something lying on the ground beside her. A familiar powder blue. And blood, now crusted and dark, almost the color of the mud around it. And blond hair, now greasy and tangled and matted with pine needles and leaves. *My body.*

I gasp. "Vi. What are you doing with that?" But it's obvious what she is doing. She's moving it toward the Outfitters, not away from it, not where it can be buried in these vast woods and safely disappear forever. She's bringing it to where the heart of the search party will be, where it will likely be buzzing with people.

She wants them to find my body.

Maybe she always wanted me dead, too, because one thing is clear. She wants me to stay that way.

CHAPTER TWENTY-ONE

"**W**hat are you doing?" I shout at her, but she doesn't listen. She grabs handfuls of greasy green hair and begins to drag my lifeless body through the mud. She's so tiny, but when I reach for her, her elbow jabs between my ribs. It doesn't hurt, but the little girl's force shocks me. Her eyes narrow to slits. She opens her mouth only a sliver, and black filth drizzles out. I know that if she could, she'd be hissing at me to get away. I put my hand on hers, trying to pry her fingers up, but the hair is wound tightly through them. All I can manage to do is pull up a few strawlike strands that break apart in my hands. I grab the hair closer to the scalp and yank in the other direction. A whole lock of hair at the crown of the head rips free in a series of sickening pops, like a seam splitting, leaving a pinkish-gray bald spot there. *That's me,* I think, wincing at the bloody clump of hair in my hands, and am so shocked for the moment that I'm not prepared for what comes next. She lunges at me, throwing me on my back and knocking all the air out of my lungs. When I recover from the shock, she's straddling my waist and holding a finger up to her muddy lips. *Quiet.*

I struggle to move, but it's useless. I'm pinned to the ground. This little girl, not four feet tall, has *pinned me to the ground*. She looks over her shoulder and before I can form another plan of escape, I hear the swish of feet along the grass. Someone is coming. I strain to see over the little girl's shoulder, but can only make out a faint glow. *Jack.* I swallow when I hear his voice. "I'm going to wring that little brat's neck." He stops, points his head to the sky, and shouts, so loud it nearly shakes the trees, "Do you hear that? I'm going to wring your neck!" And then he continues on. Once he's moved on, I exhale. She moves off of me and bends over the body again.

"Wait," I say, finally understanding. "You want my body to be found so that my mother can't bring me back to life. You don't want Jack to become ruler, either, do you?"

She wrinkles her nose and shakes her head.

I lean over and press my eyes into my knees. "All right. I'm totally confused."

There's another sound, nothing more than the crack of a branch in the distance, but Vi startles like a doe, stilling, her eyes filling once more with fear. She looks around and grabs a branch, then begins to scrawl something in the soft dirt. I watch each letter as it's produced, eager to find some answer to the mystery, but what she writes makes no sense, even when it's right in front of me, etched in mud.

Not Jack.

"What?" I shrug. "Then who?"

She stands and moves close to me, and for a moment I'm afraid, and the next moment I'm embarrassed for feeling that way in front of an eight-year-old. But I can still feel her inexplicably enormous weight on my waist pushing my back into the ground. When she grabs my hand, not at all gently, I don't know what to expect. Suddenly the world dims and I'm floating through a blur. When the world comes into focus, after a moment, things look strangely muted again, like they did when I was alive. My body is gone. Vi is gone, although, oddly, I can feel the intense pressure of her hand on mine. I swivel my head around and at once it's obvious I'm not in the same place I'd been in a second ago. The pines are gone, and now I'm surrounded mostly by leafy trees. The ground is no longer covered in pine needles; instead, I'm up to my ankles in muddy water. There is a smell in the air, like burning coal from a grill. Each way I turn, I see nothing but trees.

Before I can panic, a voice greets my ears. Out of nowhere. I see the girl, Vi, coming down the path, skipping. This time, she's different. Her pink dress is clean and unwrinkled, her shoes are unscuffed. She is singing a nursery rhyme about a man who lived in the moon, and I know right away that I have slipped into one of my visions. But what a vision! Unlike before, it is so real, I feel I can almost reach out and touch her. She even smiles at me, like she can see me there. But suddenly there is another voice. Angry. "You took them from me!"

Another person comes into view. Lannie, wearing the familiar white dress, but what is unfamiliar is the way her lip curls in hate as she storms after Vi. Vi turns, her eyes wide with fear. "I'll give them to you," she says in a voice I don't recognize. I realize I don't recognize it because I've never heard it, but it's sweet, soft, and so full of fear I want to grab her and hug her to me. Protect her. She bends over and begins to roll her sock down as Lannie says, "They're silk stockings, you know. For women. They're not kneesocks, like babies like you wear."

I stare at Lannie. I remember how she taunted me before, when we played, but it was always good-natured. It was always just fun, wasn't it? She'd never done anything horrible to me. Not at all. Then I turn in time to see Vi lift her foot out of her white shoe. She loses her balance and her foot touches the dirty forest floor.

"Look what you're doing! You're getting them all muddy! And I just bought them!"

After some more struggling, Vi manages to take both stockings off. She slips her bare feet into her knee-highs and shoes and holds the white stockings out to her sister. Lannie takes a step forward, and for a glimmer of a second before she reaches out, I see the fear in Vi's face morph into defiance. Vi throws the stockings to the ground and grinds them into the mud with the sole of her shoe. She smiles triumphantly, but it only lasts for a single instant before Lannie begins shrieking loudly enough to pierce eardrums. She lunges at Vi, screaming, "You brat! You're always in my things!" and it doesn't help when she reaches for the stockings and slips in the mud. Vi makes the mistake of laughing. I know it is a mistake and yet there is nothing I can do to stop it. I know the outcome.

They struggle in the mud. The little girl is small and bony, not strong and nearly fully grown like Lannie. It's not long before Lannie has handfuls of her little sister's long brown hair. They both fall to the ground in a heap of mud and grunts and once-crisp Sunday clothing. Vi presses her muddy palm against her sister's face, flattening her nose, trying to push her away, but it's no use. Lannie grabs her by the back of the neck and pushes her down against the forest floor. Harder, harder . . .

Then she straightens and, blinking away mud, her sister's handprint still upon her face, picks up the stockings. The forest is grave-quiet as she stands, and at first I want to run when she turns to me, but it's the same as with Justin and Angela: she doesn't see me. She walks through me, swiping a stray lock of hair behind her ear. I stare at the motionless body whose face I cannot see—so tiny, so vulnerable—tears welling in my eyes. But before they can spill over, something moves behind the trees. I wipe my eyes and strain to see a figure in the dark canopy of leaves, but I already know very well who it is. Trey.

He's the one. Get him.

It wasn't a boy who said that. It was a young woman. Lannie. She said it to Jack. She made him kill Trey, because of what he witnessed. Because he witnessed this.

Lannie did this.

I pull away from Vi's hand and I'm shuddering. "Oh my

God. It's Lannie. Lannie is my relation? She's the one in line to become Mistress of the Waters?"

Vi nods.

"She had Jack kill Trey . . . and then what?" I ask, but I already know. I hear the sound perfectly—*sleesh . . . sleesh . . . sleesh*—and the next words come to me right away. *I did everything you asked of me.* That was Jack.

I can see the whole scene so perfectly now. Jack, poor, gangly little Jack, whose pants never fit quite right and who never had any real friends, let alone girlfriends. Lannie was the first girl who'd taken any interest in him. He was easily her servant. I could see him, begging in the moonlight, begging the girl he worshipped for his life. *Please don't. I did everything you asked of me.* "But you are not a real man," Lannie spat at him. "You were going to tell everyone our secret. You couldn't keep your mouth shut." And she brought that ax down. She brought it down and killed him, too. I could see the blood coursing over his forehead, his eyes staring up through the tree branches, at the silver moon.

You become what you wanted most when you were alive. Of course. Now I know exactly why I was attracted to Jack. After being humiliated by women all his life, the one thing he wanted was to be adored by them.

"What happened to Lannie? She was caught?"

Vi strings up a pretend noose and makes like she's hanging herself.

I think of the bruises on Lannie's neck, of how I found her hanging from trees whenever we played hide-and-seek. All this time, it's been Lannie. But does it even matter? Whether it's Lannie or Jack, neither of them can become ruler. And I can't destroy an entire kingdom over my mistakes. Vi's right. We need to drag my body back to the Outfitters. We need it to be found.

CHAPTER TWENTY-TWO

When I reach for the body, Vi makes a move like she's going to try to topple me again, but I jump back before she can touch me. "Relax. I'm helping you," I explain. "Let's pick it up, though. I'll take the head."

I slide my arms under it, trying not to look, but the feeling alone is enough to make me want to throw up. This can*not* be happening. My hair is already brittle, and the whole back of my jacket is damp, yet pieces are crumbling off, either mud or dried blood. I steal a look at my face; my eyes are closed, but my mouth is slightly open, and I realize that I don't look dead, merely asleep. I squeeze my eyes shut and hoist the body up to my waist, and Vi does the same. I wondered why, with all her strength, she was having such a hard time dragging my body, but now I know. I weigh a ton. My clothes are probably waterlogged and my hair must be harboring twenty pounds of mud. It smells like wet leaves. I choke and cough and bury my face in my shoulder so I don't breathe in the smell as we begin to move toward the building. It's hidden from view, and though I know it's not far, after ten steps I feel light-headed. But Vi moves on, a determined look on her face, and so I keep going until the red cedar front of the Outfitters is visible among the trees. Vi must see it, too, because she picks up the pace and I struggle to keep up with her.

We break out of the woods, near the service entry to the building. I'm about to say that this looks like a good place to dump the body when a voice calls, "Stop!" I know who it is before I turn. Trey. At once he's beside me. He doesn't touch me, just stares at me long and hard. "What in the Sam Hill do you think you're doing?"

"What does it look like I'm doing?" I say, not making eye contact. "We're leaving the body near the Outfitters. So it can be found."

He opens his mouth to speak, but he's so furious that all he does is shake. Finally, he takes a breath and exhales slowly, and a Zenlike calm washes over him. "Kiandra. Didn't we just . . . That's a bad idea, and you know it."

"Oh, and destroying your entire kingdom is a good idea?" I shoot back, putting the body down so roughly that my shirt gets caught on a branch and rips, exposing the strap of my lacy black bra. By the time I realize how stupid it is, I've already reached down and made myself more presentable. Like someone finding my dead body would think, *Her bra is showing!*

He sighs. "This is exactly why I didn't want to tell you the whole story," he mutters, running his hands through his hair. "You're stubborn."

"Maybe you can, but I would never be able to live knowing my mistake caused pain for so many people. No way. Sorry," I say, turning my back on him.

But I can feel his eyes staring through me. "I know what this is about," he says. "Your momma. You think you got to go against everything she tells you, or else you're afraid you'll start forgiving her. Maybe she *deserves* to be forgiven."

"Enough with worshipping my mom!" I shout, turning back to him. I want to strangle him. "It's getting really old."

He looks down at the ground. "About that . . . I spent a lot of time doing things I shouldn't have. That's why my shine is still strong. Your mom should've punished me but she let me go. She saved my hide. So call it pathetic if you will." He shrugs. "I call it honor."

"I'm sorry about that," I whisper. "I didn't mean to call you that."

He motions me to follow him, and at first I don't want to leave the body, but I suppose off on this path, not twenty yards from civilization, is a good a place as any. It's not as if we can parade the body into the front lobby. I rub my hands on my jeans and walk after him, first toward the river, then around, toward the picnic benches outside the Outfitters. It's busy here. People I've never seen before are milling about with serious faces. Some are walking out through the woods. Everyone seems hyperalert. Is this for me?

Trey says to me, very softly, "I know your momma hurt you. If you want to stay mad at her, it's up to you. You ain't got to do nothing for her if you don't want to."

I'm about to say thank you, to explain that, really, I know I should forgive her, but that I just need time. It's like spending a decade loving the color blue, only to suddenly realize my favorite color is red—it doesn't seem real or right to change so soon. But then I notice that he's staring at something between the trees, something away from the river, toward the road. I follow his gaze and, among the police cars, see a very familiar gray Honda Civic, and that's when the world stops for me. The first thing I think of is how I spilled chocolate ice cream, speckled with rainbow-colored bits, on the front seat not two hours after he picked the car up from the dealer, and how he laughed and wiped it up and said, "Nice job, Sprinkles."

My dad.

Trey hitches a thumb toward the man sitting behind the steering wheel, knuckles white. "You can't undo this decision, Kiandra," Trey says. "So even if you don't want to think on your momma, you might want to think on him."

CHAPTER TWENTY-THREE

It's like the world suddenly shifts, and all the brilliance of this new world fades to darker than the old. In seconds, the allure, the beauty of this place is gone.

I was deluding myself. I'd gotten so good at forcing him out of my mind during the rafting trip—too good. But it's so easy to commit to something life-altering when you're not in the presence of the person whose life you're going to alter the most. And in a blur, every moment I've spent with him, no matter how trivial, flashes in front of my eyes, carrying weight it never did before. The same words echo in my ears: *You're my everything. You're my everything.* Suddenly I'm dizzy. Trey notices me losing my balance and props me up before I can slump to the ground, a defeated mass. Just like my father, who, behind the wheel of his Civic, looks so small and alone.

I turn to Vi, but words won't come out. There's a crushing, suffocating pain in my chest, like my heart is breaking into a thousand pieces. Finally, something comes, the only thing I can manage. "I'm sorry."

My dad steps out of the car and he's wearing his trademark wrinkled tweed blazer and L.L.Bean hiking boots. His hair is sticking up, which is a usual thing in the morning before he showers. He has a stack of flyers in his hands; I can see the word MISSING in bright red on top. There's a picture underneath and I bet with everything I am that it's the one of me last Christmas, wearing the Santa hat he always forced on me. I look about ten in the picture, which is why he loved it and put it on his desk at school. I'm sure that in the next half hour, half the trees in Forks will have that picture tacked to their trunks.

I turn to Trey. "What do you want me to do?" I ask, ignoring Vi's expression. She begins to shake her head, first slowly, then building up momentum.

"We got to get that body in the boat," Trey says. "We got to take it back." When Trey reaches for the body, Vi moves to block his way. The way she stares at him, she looks seven feet tall.

I whisper to her, "I can't leave my dad. I'm sorry. I have to go back."

Her face, marred with dirt, doesn't change. She crosses her arms in front of her ruffled dress, and despite the ruffles and lace, she looks fierce, like an ancient warrior. I'm surprised that with her strength and bravery, she could be so afraid of someone like her sister, Lannie. Suddenly I realize something. "That's what you wanted," I say to Vi, softly at first. "You become the thing that you wanted most in life. When she held you down in the mud, you wanted to be stronger than her. And you are."

She just stares at me, her face stone.

"And don't you see? She was in line to become Mistress. You're her *sister*. You're a member of *our* family. That means that you have the same powers we do. Right?" I turn to Trey. "We can fight her ourselves. Right?"

Trey laughs. "Whoa, cowboy. You ain't fighting nobody. Not if you want to get home."

"Okay, but *she* can, right? She's more powerful than Lannie, so . . ."

Vi is shaking her head vehemently.

I stare at her. "What are you saying? I wish you could talk, already."

Suddenly she begins to choke. She doubles over, but when she straightens, her mouth is clear. And suddenly I don't wish it anymore, because the next thing that comes out is a whine. "I am not doing that," she pouts. "Never ever ever." Then she realizes what she's done, and grins for half a second before she sneers at me. "Took you long enough, Miss All-Powerful. I've been begging you to do that for only *a million years* or something."

I step back. "Wait. What just . . . Did I do that?"

Vi rolls her eyes and wipes the remaining mud from her chin. "For a Mistress, you're really not that smart." She leans against a tree, pouting.

Brat. I almost wish I hadn't done that. Whatever it is I

did, which *I don't know*. I stare at my hands. Did I do anything with them? No, I clearly remember them being in the pockets of my jacket. All I'd done was say that I wished she could talk. I turn to Trey, confused. "I just say it, and it happens?"

He shakes his head. "We went over this. You don't even got to say it. You just got to want it."

Right. I do remember him saying something like that. I've wanted so many things, but I never just got them. I try to think of something, but nothing comes to mind.

She shrugs. "Anyway, don't ask me to do that. To my sister. I can't fight her."

"Don't give her that, little girl. I seen what you can do," Trey says to her. Then to me he whispers, "Look, she's eight. She don't get things like you and I do. Her sister is the only family she knows. She don't want to be alone."

She rolls her eyes. "I can hear every word you're saying!" she shrieks. "You think you know so much because you're older than me?" She stares at me. "I've been around *years* longer than you. I know a thing or two."

"Your sister isn't nice to you. She killed you," I say.

She looks from Trey to me and crosses her arms. Her face sours.

"Then why were you trying to hide my body?" I ask.

Trey studies her and says, "Because if her sister becomes Mistress, she ain't gonna be just her sister." And it makes sense. If her sister can weaken my mother and become

Mistress, then she'll be busy with other things. Vi won't have her sister. "You afraid of being on your own, is that it?"

Vi doesn't answer, so I just shake my head. "Right. Her brain's still eight."

Trey shrugs. "That don't mean nothing. No fun being alone, whatever age you are." He walks in front of the body and stands there, arms crossed. "We're taking this body across the river, little girl, whether you like it or not. So scram."

She stares at him, her nostrils flaring with rage. At first I think she's going to challenge him. Instead, she turns and runs back down the path.

"You shouldn't have done that," I say. "She's going to come back and bring her sister."

He says, "You forget. This is what they want us to do." He must realize I'm about to feel guilty again, because he squeezes my hand. "Kiandra. Everything'll be okay. Now let's get out of here."

CHAPTER TWENTY-FOUR

By the time we get back to the rowboat, the sun, orange and lazy, is sliding down behind the tall pines. Trey's quiet as he rows across the river. Though we're facing each other and our knees are only a foot apart, he rows with his head down, never looking at me. I watch the muscles of his arms strain as he rows the boat, which is the only indication he's working at all. His breath comes slow and steady, and the rowing seems so effortless for him, like he must do it all the time.

Trey exhales and he arches his arms back, and the oars smack against the surface of the water, propelling us forward. "Your boyfriend must be real worried about you." I can tell the gears in his head are turning, though, because he moves his mouth in about a hundred different ways but no words come out. Finally, he says, "When I was alive I thought I'd have all sorts of time for that kind of thing. Girls, I mean."

"You didn't have a girlfriend?" I ask.

"Nah. Not even close." Trey shrugs. "Thought I'd have the

time. But guess we never have as much time as we think we're going to. Missed out on a lot."

From the look on his face, a sad, distant longing, it's obvious he's thinking of something in particular. "What do you regret the most?"

I think he's going to say something about his mom. Instead, he gives me a sheepish look. "Well, I ain't asking for nothing, but I wished I'd kissed a girl."

I raise my eyebrows. He looks away. I feel heat in my face and he looks over his shoulder, away from me, but I know he's blushing, too. Talk about awkward. "Is that all?" I finally say.

"Well, maybe if you done it before, ain't no big deal. But I ain't, and I had a whole mess of years to think on it. And yeah, it may be a little thing to you, but it's not when someone's had that long to think it over."

"No, I didn't mean to . . . I wasn't making fun of you. I just thought you'd say something else. Something about your mom."

"Yeah, well. I hate dying in a way that she didn't know what happened to me, but that wasn't my doing. But kissing. Hell. I could have done that. I could have kissed the socks off a dozen girls at school. They all gave me looks. I was pretty hot stuff, I should imagine."

I burst out laughing. "Oh yeah?"

He sticks out his lower lip, then sucks it in. "Well, maybe back then. Maybe girls these days want something else. I don't know. Girls always kind of befuddled me."

That word makes me laugh even more. "Befuddled?"

"Yeah. What? That not a word they use these days? Girls are befuddling. With a capital B. It means that one day they like the rain and the next they're crying about it. They don't know what they want but they expect you to know it. Be. Fud. Ling."

"I don't think girls are befuddling. I think guys are. What's with the whole wanting-to-be-outdoors-in-subzero-temperatures? Cooking on an open fire? Who wants to be at one with nature? I'd rather not be, thank you very much." I cross my arms over my chest. "I mean, hunting? Fishing? Gross."

"You used to fish. You never minded holding them wriggling worm bodies in your hands then. You *liked* getting mussed up. You used to scrape up the fish scales and put them on your thighs and watch the sun dance on them."

"Yeah, but I . . ." "Grew up" is on my tongue, but it doesn't come out, because suddenly I'm transported to that day I met him, on the river outside my house. I didn't catch a fish then, didn't hold one in my hands. Sure, I'd caught plenty before, and I was so angry at him for catching so many and letting them go. But how did he know I liked the mess? How did he know what I did with the scales? "You . . . watched me?"

"You're the next Mistress. I'm a guide. Of course I watched you. Up till you left. Then I couldn't watch you no more."

"Oh, right," I say, feeling disappointed, though I'm not sure why.

He laughs a little to himself. "You know, the funny thing

was, I had a picture of you in my mind, all this time, of what you would look like grown up. And it was right."

"That's . . . Really?" I wonder what I look like to him. I wonder if he's disappointed that I don't like to fish anymore.

"Most days I wondered if I'd ever see you again. Thought you were gone for good. But I'm glad I got the chance to before I . . ." He looks away. "I'm glad I got the chance to."

He grips the oars tighter, and I realize that there's something on his mind. Something he's not telling me. "Before you what?" I ask.

"Ain't nothing." And by the way he says it, I know it's something. Something big.

By this point we're at the shore. He jumps out of the boat and pushes it onto land.

I grab his arm. "You have to tell me. You're sending me back and telling me not to get involved. But I *am* involved."

He throws the oars back into the boat. "You're a Mistress. We protect our Mistresses. End of story."

"But you said it's going to weaken my mother if she gives me life. How's that going to protect her?"

"It would weaken her, yeah. But just as some things weaken her, other things can make her strong again. And I know you don't get my allegiance to your momma, but I got to do this. For the kingdom."

I stand there staring at him, uncomprehending. "Do . . . what, exactly?"

"I've been here long enough as it is. I made this decision

long time ago. I'm giving her my power. My shine. I got a lot to give, you've noticed."

"But . . . what? And then what happens to you?"

"I move on. Somewhere else." He's silent for a minute, studying me. "Look, Kiandra, I been here too long. And this, it's a good thing. Something I should've done a while ago."

"But so you're saying that when I finally do come back here, as Mistress . . . you won't be here?"

He raises an eyebrow. "That matter?"

"Well . . . I mean, yes. I like having a friend here."

I don't realize until he shakes it that he's been extending his hand to me, to help me out of the boat. Even with his support, I stumble awkwardly, my boots sinking up to the laces in mud. Somehow, though Vi, with her unnatural strength, and I had a hard time carrying the body, Trey is able to heft it over his shoulder like it's nothing. My hair, greenish and greasy, hangs down past his knees, its ends nearly scraping the ground.

I hear footsteps, and my mother is running down the path. "Hurry," she says. "We have to do this now."

Sure, Mom, you wouldn't want to spend one more minute with me than you have to. I step forward and mumble, "Fine. What do I have to do?"

She stands in front of me. "Oh, Kiandra, it isn't like that. Your father moved you away because he was afraid of losing you. He knew that the river consumed me, and that it called to me, and that I had visions that would wake me up screaming at night. He must have seen the same signs in you, and he couldn't stand to have it happen to you, too. But what he doesn't know is that it saved me. Coming here, I knew I could still be with you. You can see visions of us on the river, right?"

"Yes, but—" Suddenly I understand what she's saying. I cover my mouth with my hand. "You mean . . ."

"But your father took you away. Now, I don't blame him, but I wished every day that he hadn't, and that you would come back to me. What I'm saying is that you don't have to be alone. If you come to the river, I will find a way to see you."

Tears spring to my eyes. She puts her hands on my shoulders and leans in to kiss my forehead.

She puts a hand on my forehead, like she used to do to check whether I had a fever. Her skin is clammy and cold, everything I remember. But suddenly I am feeling feverish and dizzy and breathless all at once. The edges of my sight blur and soon all the colors are swirling together, like some child's finger painting. Then everything dims to a murky black, and all I can feel and hear is the beating of my heart.

Maybe it's only seconds later that I spring upright, still feeling dizzy as things settle around me. I'm in the boat again. Trey is rowing, his back to me. Black water, topped with yellow foam, is swirling around us. The sky is thick with clouds, as if a storm is threatening. I feel different, but it's a familiar difference. My heart flutters in my chest. I lift the folds of my jacket and check my stomach. No wound. I know what this is. This is life.

"I'm alive again?" I ask softly.

Trey doesn't stop rowing.

"Where are we going?"

"Where do you think? I'm rowing you ashore, and you got to get to your daddy and get away from here." He turns and gives me a hard stare. "Got it?"

"Yes," I say. "But what about—"

"None of that," he groans. "You need to get. Don't worry about the rest."

"But what are you going to do?"

"I'm going to get back to your mom and give her my shine. That'll restore some of her power. Otherwise she won't be strong enough to stop Lannie."

"But . . . Oh." Somehow this tugs at my heart in ways I didn't think existed. I can't help but ask, "But then you . . . I'm never going to see you again, right?"

He rolls his eyes at me. "I told you, quit worrying. There ain't nothing you can do. This is the way it needs to be. You go on back to that boyfriend of yours."

"He's not, anymore," I mumble. "It's a long story."

He pulls the boat ashore and stands, hands on hips, waiting for me. I sit there, stunned. Why do I get to live while everyone else suffers? It seems so unfair. I'm about to tell him this when he speaks.

"You ain't getting any more alive. Now get."

I climb out of the boat, feeling strange on my feet, like every step is unsure and my ankles might give out at any moment. I'm cold again, so I wrap my arms around my body. "Thank you," I say softly, feeling like I should say more, do more. So that is why I open my arms and reach them around him, pulling him into a hug.

After a moment, his body relaxes, and I feel his arms around me, too. It feels nice. I know he needs to be going, but I don't want to let go. I press the side of my face against his chest, and he must be reading my mind because he says, "Aw, Kiandra, don't you worry."

I tilt my head back and he's looking down at me, trying to smile, but I can see the heaviness in his eyes. So I push myself up on the tips of my toes and press my lips against his. Mine are cold and his are so blazing hot, but it's not his warmth that makes me cling to him. It's something else. Maybe it's that in all my time with Justin I never felt this complete bliss, his body making me feel whole. Trey holds me closer, his lips on mine, and soon everything else is forgotten and we're lost in each other. Finally, breathless, I pull away from his mouth, and he nibbles along my jaw until he finds my earlobe. "Kiandra," he whispers, and then he says something that sounds very much like "I love you."

But before I have a chance to respond, to look into his eyes and see if he really meant it, the world dims. And everything disappears.

CHAPTER TWENTY-FIVE

I blink awake, only to find myself lying in the soft pine needles. It's dark and bitingly cold, and the only sound is the rushing of water. My body is numb from the cold. Cold! I feel cold. I pull up my shirt and run my hand along the smooth skin of my belly. I sit up quickly and realize the fingers of my other hand are wrapped around something. I open them, and in the moonlight I can just make it out. A wilted flower petal.

Flowers? From where?

And suddenly it hits me. The Outfitters, and me swaying with Justin under the swirling disco lights. The corsage he gave me, crumpled and wilted.

I gasp. I ran away, and I slipped on the rocky embankment, and . . . then what?

Was it all just . . .

Could it have been . . .

And when I think of everything that has happened to me in the past twenty-four hours—somehow being stabbed, dying, meeting my mother, searching for my body, kissing

Trey—I know it. I bring my hand to my lips, and they're frozen, stone. Of course. Of *course* none of that happened.

I stand up and start to run, and stop when a jagged pain rips through the back of my head. I hit my head, passed out cold. Who knows how long I've been out here, wherever *here* is? I'm surrounded by nothing but trees and inky darkness. I need to get to the Outfitters. I need to see my dad. Justin. Angela.

Because I can barely feel my legs, I'm nowhere near as graceful as I'd been in my dream—*was* it a dream? I stumble over the rocks, then fall to my knees and feel a rock dig into my flesh. *Now* I feel my legs. The pain makes me see fireworks. Fireworks. The bright colors of my dreamworld are gone. The beauty of the way everything struck me as if I were seeing it for the first time. Now everything is dull again, heartbreakingly so. I try not to concentrate on it as I find my way up the embankment, and yet that's all I can see.

That is, until Trey appears before me.

He's a ghost, I know, and for the first time, he looks that way. He's tinged with blue, faded, yet so perfect. His face may not be clean-shaven, but his wounds are gone. He smiles at me.

I hear his voice, clear inside my head. *Everything is all right now. I'm moving on. Wanted to tell you something, though. I shouldn't have denied it.*

"Kiandra!" a voice calls. It's one I haven't heard in centuries. I whirl around. Justin. He's standing at the top of the embankment, the hood of a rain slicker hiding his face. But even though I can't see most of him, I can tell he's stricken with relief and amazement. He starts to navigate his way down the rocky ledge, but by now I'm reaching for something that is just out of my grasp. Trey is walking away, in that same lazy, carefree way I've come to know.

"Trey!" I shout. "No! Just—"

Justin moves closer, ignoring my plea. "What?" he's asking. He has his arms out, ready to envelop me, to pull me close to his big, strong body the way he has a thousand times. "What's wrong?"

Justin clutches me to him, and in the music of his heartbeat, I watch Trey walk to the river. I wish he'd just look back, but he doesn't stop, doesn't even falter. Everything is still, so still, except him. I need to run for him, to grab him, to tell him to come back. When I push myself away from Justin, there is no sound but the whistle of the wind, no movement but the dance of the leaves in the trees. Justin whispers, "You're in shock. Let's get you inside, okay?"

I push against his body with such violence that he steps back. "No!" I scream, but the second I do, Trey disappears, leaving nothing but an outline in my memory. I blink again and again, but he is gone. I turn to Justin. It's him. He's lured me back to reality, to his world, when I need to be in the other one. I need to be with the dead. But as I look around helplessly, I realize I have no idea how to get back. I clasp my hands over my mouth. "Oh my God. He's gone."

He moves closer, tentative, and scans through the pines. "Who is *he*?"

"Leave me," I whisper into my hands. I don't know how long I've been crying, but my palms are slick and salty with tears.

Suddenly a fireball bursts in the distance. I don't even look at it, almost as if I expected it, and yet I don't know where it came from. Justin steps back, his mouth forming an O. "What the—"

He starts to take a step toward it, but as I'm moaning "Please, can't you leave me?" another fireball bursts behind us. It rocks Justin, and he steadies himself as I remain still. The rain begins to fall steadily now, and the fire melts to nothing, but Justin surveys the area, and I know that in all the years he's been here, he's never seen anything like it. But still he won't leave.

"What the hell? We've got to get out of here, Ki. *Now*."

"Leave me," I beg, knowing there will be another eruption, possibly closer, if he stays. I don't know how I know, but I know.

But I can't expect him to leave. He's just found me. Instead of obeying, he narrows his eyes. "Wait. You've been missing for nearly twenty-four hours and now you're telling me you don't want to be found? Jesus, Ki, did you do this on purpose? Because of me?"

I simply stare at the spot where Trey once stood. I can't comprehend what Justin is saying. Because of him? Why because of him? Everything from this world is strange, like walking into a foreign country. I turn to him as he tries to put his arm around me. Even he looks different. His arm around me feels different, heavier. Wrong.

"No, I didn't do this on purpose," I whisper, because I know that if I admit I did, I'd have to acknowledge that everything that happened to Trey is my fault.

And it is.

Why can't I see him? Is he gone? Off to the next place? Away to where I will never see him again?

Tears flood my eyes again. I start to speak, to explain, but I don't know how to explain this. Justin puts a warm hand over mine, and it's only when my hand starts to sting in his that I realize my limbs are frozen. He says, "You're like ice. You can explain later. Let's go back. Your dad is waiting for you."

My dad. It's those words that lift me. Justin helps me to my feet, and they feel like they're tethered to the ground with elastic bands as I walk unsteadily toward the path that will lead us to the rest of civilization. To my old life. How can it be that it's only been a day since I've been part of it? I slump against Justin, and the one thing that feels familiar is how effortlessly he piles me into his arms. In the rhythm of his footfalls, I'm lulled to sleep.

CHAPTER TWENTY-SIX

When I wake, I'm in the middle of a big, fluffy bed piled high with white comforters and pillows. It's Angela's cabin, bright lacquered log walls covered in rustic frames holding wilderness scenes, windows open to the green pine boughs outside. I prop myself up on my elbows and inspect my white nightgown, unable to recall where or when I got such a strange piece of clothing. As I'm contemplating the contents of the bag I dragged up here, there's a creaking in the doorway, and Trey appears.

He's perfect. His face may not be clean-shaven, but his wounds are gone. He smiles at me.

This isn't real, is it? I don't say it. I don't need to say it. He understands every word. He nods and slips a hand behind my neck, pulling me up to him in the most real kiss I've ever felt in my life. His lips burn mine, etching a permanent impression there. When he pulls away, I reach for him, wanting more, and when my hands graze his skin, I hear his voice, clear inside my head.

I'm moving on. Wanted to tell you something, though. I shouldn't have denied it.

No, I say. *Don't. Say it to me when you're holding me for real. Because you're not moving on. I won't let you.*

You're not moving on. My eyes flicker open. Unlike in my dream, this time the room is bathed in darkness. There is no strip of light under the door; the only brightness comes from the moon peeking through the pines. It's late. My skin feels clammy, all except for my lips, which still burn from the kiss.

I won't let you.

I stare at my hands, wondering what I could have meant. And all at once I remember the fireballs in the forest. The bright explosions that bewildered me and Justin.

They were mine. I created them myself. *With my powers.*

I pull off the covers and I'm wearing only a long thermal T-shirt, but I don't think about the cold. I run barefoot down the stairs and out into the night as a chorus of owls hoots a welcome. I rush to the darkness, letting it envelop me, no longer afraid of what it might bring. I do not fear what is out here. Somehow, even in the darkness, I can find the place I'd last seen him. *Take me there, please. Take me to him.*

"Trey," I whisper.

And suddenly he is lying before me, in the clearing, the moonlight making the sweat glisten on his forehead and bare chest. It's the only thing that glows, because there is no shine left in him. His eyes are closed, but they flicker a bit when I approach him.

"Hey, you," he mumbles.

"Hey," I say, drawing his head onto my bare knees.

"I thought you were gone for good," he says.

I wipe a tear from my eyes. "I thought the same thing about you."

I think he tries to shrug, because his body tenses. "Soon."

I shake my head. "Look, did you really mean what you . . . didn't say?" I realize it's stupid. I dreamed it. But there's no time for it now. "Do you love me? Because I think I love you. Actually, I know I do."

His mouth spreads into a smile. "Since I first met you. You and your attitude and your fancy-shmancy fishing pole."

"What? Are you serious?" I sputter through tears. I can barely see him.

"You think I did all that for your momma because of *her*? It was for *you*, kid. Always you." He reaches up to touch my face, but his hand falls back. I know he is too weak.

I know I don't have much time. "I guess you were right about me. I am stronger than I'd thought," I whisper, wiping my cheeks with the back of my hand. His forehead is strangely warm when I press my fingers against it. "And there's this thing I think I can do."

Just let this work, I pray as I close my eyes and concentrate on the one thing I know I really want.

EPILOGUE

FOUR MONTHS LATER

I whisper my secrets to the river. I know she can hear them. I know that she loves me, and that I will see her again. I blow a kiss across the waves, and I know, I just know, that on the other side, she will be there to catch it. That she has always been there.

And that the river always gives us a chance to wipe away our past mistakes and start anew.

I look up to the branches hanging over me. It's a perfect day in September, warm but not hot, and the leaves and branches are still vibrant green with life. Up the embankment, Justin and Angela are setting up the tent. Yes, a tent. We're going fishing. And I was the one who suggested it. Mostly because homecoming is next weekend and I've made tuxedos and high heels mandatory. I think of my boyfriend in a tuxedo instead of dirty jeans and my heart begins to flutter.

I climb up to where Justin and Angela have just about

everything under control. Angela and Justin are piling kindling, piece by piece. They are so cute together, it makes me wonder why they never got together sooner. Oh, right, there was a little something standing in the way. Me.

Angela looks up at me and wipes the sweat from her brow, clearly excited. I know the outdoors makes her a little giddy, but I've really never seen her as happy as she's been for the past few months. "You know, scary story time is *on*," she says. "I've got a good one, Honey Bunches, so you'd better grab your teddy bear."

"I'm right here," a voice says behind me. It's Trey, and he's gnawing on a Slim Jim and grinning down at me. He is now addicted to them. Apparently they didn't have them back in his old life. He's being corrupted by a lot things, though. Wii, Hostess Sno Balls, the Fishing Channel. He's gained weight, which, even though it makes him more of a teddy bear, has also made him better-looking.

He's also had to get used to wearing shoes. When he walks to meet us, he stumbles a bit in his hiking boots, then straightens himself. He looks from one of us to the other. "What's going on?" He holds up the Slim Jim. "Okay that I swiped this from the food bag?"

It's only then I realize that Angela is also staring at him, openmouthed. I nudge her to stop. She says, "Sure, knock yourself out." Then, when he walks away, she mutters, "God, he is so hot. Where did you find him, again?"

I grin at her. "You're not going to steal *him* from me, too?"

She grins back. Angela the boyfriend stealer. She spent

weeks apologizing to me, until I finally got it through her head that I was okay with it. More than okay. I was happy. And it wasn't just because I had Trey. Some things are just meant to be.

As the sun begins to slide behind the trees, Trey puts his arms around me and pulls me close. When he says "I love you," I know that this, us, is one of those things.

"Who's going to make the fire?" Angela asks.

"I'm on it," I say, holding up two sticks.

Angela and Justin look at each other and burst out laughing. "I'll believe that when I see it," Justin mumbles.

"Prepare to be amazed," I say, crouching over the fire pit.

I concentrate on wanting it. Two minutes later, a good-sized fire is crackling in the pit. My cousin and my ex-boyfriend exchange glances, sufficiently impressed. Trey leans over me and whispers, "I call that cheating, kid."

I grin. "How is it cheating, using my innate Mistress abilities?"

He bows. "Oh, of course, Your Royal Highness."

When I try to smack him, he grabs my hand and pulls me into another embrace. His kiss is hotter than any fire I could make.

Later, we all sit in a circle, toasting marshmallows, and when it's time to tell stories, I'm the first to volunteer. Because I have a really good one. But this one is true, and best of all, it has a happy ending.

ABOUT THE AUTHOR

CYN BALOG fell out of the raft on her first, and only, trip down the Dead River. She is the author of *Starstruck, Sleepless,* and *Fairy Tale.* Cyn lives in Pennsylvania with her family. Visit her online at cynbalog.com.